*"Hey, don't get Darren started on women."
Jason laughed. "I think he's just sensitive.
We've been trying to find Mrs. Right for him
for ages now, and so far it's been a no go in every
situation."*

Darren shrugged. "I just don't see the purpose in dating. Maybe I have a different view of things. I guess I'm a little old-fashioned."

"Not at all." Candy looked at him and shrugged. "I think dating is a waste of time, too. It's almost like you're trying people out, one at a time. Seems kind of. . .odd."

Brooke giggled. "It's funny, hearing Darren talk about women at the dinner table. Usually it's the other way around with pilots. When they're flying they talk about women, and when they're with a woman, they talk about flying."

Jason laughed long and loud at that one. Darren felt the tips of his ears heat up, something he could never seem to control when embarrassed. He'd have to talk to Jason later about making him the brunt of every joke, especially in front of someone as pretty as Candy.

Brooke changed the direction of the conversation at that very moment. He breathed a sigh of relief as she started talking about a passenger on a recent flight, one who'd given her fits over a spilled soft drink.

Though he tried to pay attention, he found his gaze shifting back to Candy. The name suited her. She was sweet, through and through.

Hmm. Sweet. What was it he'd said to Brooke that day on the plane? *"Give me a sweet woman. That's all I'm asking for."*

Maybe. . .just maybe. . .the Lord had dropped one in his lap.

FICTION

**JANICE HANNA** (also known as Janice A. Thompson) has published over thirty books for the Christian market, most lighthearted and/or wedding themed. Working with quirky characters and story ideas suits this fun-loving author. She particularly enjoys contemporary romantic comedies. Wedding-themed books come naturally to Janice, since she's coordinated nearly a dozen weddings, including recent ceremonies/receptions for all four daughters. Most of all, she loves sharing her faith with readers and hopes they will catch a glimpse of the real "happily ever after" in her stories.

Books by Janice A. Thompson

## HEARTSONG PRESENTS
HP490—A Class of Her Own
HP593—Angel Incognito
HP613—A Chorus of One
HP666—Sweet Charity
HP667—Banking On Love
HP734—Larkspur Dreams—coauthored with Anita Higman
HP754—Red Like Crimson
HP778—The Love Song—coauthored with Anita Higman
HP786—White As Snow
HP806—Out of the Blue
HP813—Castles in the Air—coauthored with Anita Higman

Books by Janice Hanna

HP834—Salt Water Taffie

# Cotton Candy Clouds

*Janice Hanna*

*Heartsong Presents*

To my sister-in-law, Stacey Hanna, a high-flyin' pilot who somehow manages to keep her head out of the clouds.

A note from the Author:
*I love to hear from my readers! You may correspond with me by writing:*

> **Janice Hanna**
> **Author Relations**
> **PO Box 721**
> **Uhrichsville, OH 44683**

**ISBN 978-1-60260-353-0**

**COTTON CANDY CLOUDS**

*Our mission is to publish and distribute inspirational products offering exceptional value and biblical encouragement to the masses.*

PRINTED IN THE U.S.A.

## one

"Fasten your seat belt, please."

Candy Carini pushed aside her daydreams and looked up into the eyes of the flight attendant. After a cursory nod, she snapped the seat belt tight, then turned to look out the window once again. For as long as she could remember, she'd loved sitting in the window seat. Of course, her favorite place to sit these days was in the cockpit. And once she made it through the interview process at Eastway, she'd be making most of her flights from that position. If things went as planned, anyway.

As the plane taxied toward the runway, the woman in the seat next to Candy reached into her oversized purse and pulled out a piece of gum, which she extended in Candy's direction. "Would you like one?"

"Oh, sure." Candy reached for it, offering a polite smile. "Thanks. It really helps my ears during takeoff."

She unwrapped the gum and popped it into her mouth, then leaned her head against the seat and shifted her gaze out the window once again. The plane eased its way into line behind several others, and the waiting game began. In the meantime, the flight attendant began the usual safety spiel. . . a little too animated, to Candy's way of thinking. The perky blond had clearly given this speech a couple thousand times or more.

"I don't like this part," the woman next to Candy said as she pressed her purse back into place under the seat in front of her. "I guess I'm just impatient."

"Me, too," Candy agreed. "But it's like everything else in life. Good things come to those who wait." Take today, for instance. She'd had her share of waiting. Boarding her first flight in Phoenix early this morning. Making the connecting Eastway flight in Chicago a couple of hours later. And all to get to New Jersey. . .to see her family and, hopefully, acquire a new job. Yes, her patience had certainly been tried. But it would all be worth it.

"I guess you're right. Never thought of it like that." The woman went on to introduce herself as Wanda Kenner, adding, "I'll just be glad when we land in Newark. I've been missing my grandbaby something fierce. I don't get to see her nearly often enough."

Candy certainly knew what it felt like to be separated from family. She'd lived the past couple of years away from her parents and sisters.

Minutes later their 747 reached the head of the line. In the seconds before takeoff, Candy felt the usual sense of exhilaration. That feeling—that awesome, powerful feeling— reminded her once again of the call God had placed on her life: the call to fly. Since childhood she'd dreamed of soaring above the clouds, and now that dream was actually becoming a reality.

The roar of the engines sounded, and the plane began its inevitable journey faster, faster, and faster until the front end tipped up, skyward. Within seconds, the back wheels lifted and Candy found herself leaning back against the seat whispering, "We have liftoff!"

"Excuse me?" Mrs. Kenner looked at her with furrowed brow. "Were you talking to me?"

"Oh no. I was just—" Candy laughed. "Just talking to myself, really. After the takeoff. Nice and smooth."

"Ah. Wish they were all like that. The last time my husband and I came to see our grandbaby, we had the most terrifying takeoff. And the landing was worse." Mrs. Kenner proceeded to share the details with heightened enthusiasm. "We got two landings for the price of one that day."

Candy couldn't help but smile at the woman's sense of humor. "Good thing you can laugh about it," she said.

"Well, I can laugh now, but not at the time." Mrs. Kenner fanned herself with her hand. "It's a miracle we're still alive. Really."

"Wow." Candy smiled. In the days leading up to getting her pilot's license, she'd struggled through a few rough takeoffs and landings. Thankfully, she'd seen great improvement over the past few months while flying smaller planes in Arizona. Now she'd turned her sights to piloting bigger planes for Eastway. Just the idea of flying out of Newark brought a smile to her face. How wonderful it would be, to be back in Jersey once again. Close to family. Close to home.

Candy gazed out the window once more. Billows of white clouds now wrapped the plane in their embrace. The backdrop of deep blue sky behind the wispy clouds nearly took her breath away. Something about the contrast of colors always put her in mind of creation—God speaking the heavens into existence. She could almost hear it now. "Let there be light!" And there was light.

Just then, a voice came over the speaker. "Good afternoon, ladies and gentlemen. Welcome aboard Eastway Airlines flight 1403 from Chicago to Newark. This is your captain, Darren Furst. Not second, first."

A few of the passengers chuckled, but Candy rolled her eyes. Just then, the plane jerked a bit and Mrs. Kenner's eyes widened. "Oh dear."

Candy's gaze shot to the window once again. She expected to see heavier, darker clouds looming, but nothing significant jumped out at her. Certainly no reason for a rocky flight.

"Just a little turbulence, folks," the captain continued. "Keep those seat belts on until we tell you otherwise. And by the way. . .once the seat belt sign goes off, we ask you to please limit your walking to *inside* the plane, not out. When passengers walk on the wings it tends to affect our flight pattern."

A handful of passengers chuckled, but Candy did not. Turning back to the woman, she pursed her lips. "His comedic skills are great, but this isn't a stand-up show." *He needs to pay more attention to his flying skills and leave the comedy to folks on TV.*

"I've seen a lot of rocky takeoffs." Mrs. Kenner shrugged. "I'm sure he's a fine pilot."

Candy nodded. "Well yes, but—"

"We'll be flying at an altitude of thirty-five thousand feet," came the voice over the speaker, interrupting her thoughts. "Our expected arrival time in Newark is 5:52 p.m. The weather in Newark is a warm eighty-eight degrees with some broken clouds. We're hoping they'll have them fixed before we attempt to land. Now, settle back and enjoy your flight."

Candy did her best to do just that. Ignoring the chuckles around her, she reached for her MP3 player, pressed in the earplugs, and scrolled until she found the perfect worship song. *Ah. Much better.* With the soothing melody playing, she could almost relax.

Almost.

About three-quarters of the way into the song, as they continued their ascent, the plane began to tip to the right and then the left. The woman next to her reached into her purse again, pulling out a pill bottle. "I need an airsickness pill. This flight is really making me feel queasy."

"Me, too. But I'll skip the airsickness pill. They make me loopy."

"I do have to wonder about that pilot." The woman's brow wrinkled as she swallowed one of the pills with no water. "He's got to be a novice. Either that or we've got some really rough weather ahead." She fastened the top back on the bottle and put it in her purse.

"I can't do anything about the weather, but it does make me wish it was my turn in the cockpit." Candy shrugged.

"You mean you're a pilot?" The woman gave her an

admiring look. When Candy nodded, she added, "Good for you, honey. These days, women can be anything they set their minds to. When I was a girl, only men had jobs like that." She laughed. " 'Course, when I was a girl, men held most of the jobs, period. I think it's wonderful that young women today are getting out there. . .fulfilling their dreams."

"Oh, women have been flying for ages," Candy explained. "There's a great organization called Women in Aviation. I'm a member. And there's another group specifically for female pilots called the Ninety-Nines that was formed in 1929." She went on to tell the woman all about the group, and how she hoped to join after she got hired on at Eastway.

"So, your job with the airline looks hopeful?"

A smile teased the edges of Candy's lips. "Yes, I'm headed to Newark for my final interview. I took the FAA check ride last year. Passed it with no problems."

"Check ride?"

"Private pilot certification. Scary process, but I made it through."

"So you're ready to go."

She shrugged. "Well, it's not that easy. You've got to have a minimum of 250 flight hours under your belt to take the check ride. I had that. But getting my commercial license didn't mean I could fly for one of the airlines. Most require more than a thousand flight hours, and 250 of those have to be in IMC."

"IMC?" Mrs. Kenner looked confused.

"Instrument meteorological conditions. So, I've been in Arizona, building up my time flying for a cargo carrier. I worked for a little while as a skydiving pilot, too, but that was more for fun."

"Skydiving?" Mrs. Kenner grinned. "I know you probably won't believe this, but I've always had the desire to jump out of a plane." She looked out of the window as the plane gave another jolt. "Not today, of course. Unless that pilot doesn't get his act together." After another jerk, she added, "Somebody hand me a parachute."

Candy laughed. "I don't think we're quite ready for that yet. And from the looks of things, this isn't ideal jumping weather."

Mrs. Kenner leaned back against her seat and closed her eyes for a few seconds until the bumpy flight straightened itself out. When things had finally settled down, she opened one eye and peered at Candy. "So, you have enough hours to work for one of the airlines now?"

"Well, a regional carrier like Eastway," Candy explained. "Not a major airline. But eventually I hope to fly for one of the bigger companies, maybe even transatlantic flights." Just the idea sent a shiver down her spine. . .in a good way.

"Of course."

"Eastway just makes sense for now, since they fly out of Newark. My family lives in Atlantic City and I like the idea of being so close to home again." Candy went on to tell the woman about her family's candy shop on the boardwalk. Then she reached into her bag and produced a clear plastic bag of saltwater taffy in a variety of flavors. She extended it toward the woman. "My mom's always sending me sweets from our shop. Have one."

"Oh, saltwater taffy! My favorite!" The woman grabbed the bag and stared at the label. "Carini's Confections. They're on the south end of the boardwalk, right?"

"Right."

"I remember visiting that store when I was just a girl. There was a wonderful man who ran it back then." She took a light red piece of the taffy, quickly unwrapped it, and popped it into her mouth.

"That would be my grandpa Gus." Candy smiled at the memory of her grandfather. "He passed away several years ago. My parents took over the shop, but now they've retired. They're gone several months a year, traveling in their RV. My older sister, Taffie, runs the store now."

"Taffie?" The woman spoke around the wad of candy in her mouth. "Well, if that isn't clever." She paused a moment to focus on chewing. "And your name is Candy," she said after swallowing.

Candy sighed. "Yes. But don't say that too loudly, okay?" Even after years of being away from home, she still cringed at the thought of their names. Taffie, Candy, and Tangie. The three Carini sisters.

"I think it's cute." The woman gave her a wink, then licked some of the stickiness off her fingers. "So, are you going to get to see your family while you're in Newark?"

"Yes, I can't wait. My sister Taffie just got married, a little over a year ago, and she's expecting her first baby. I was there for the wedding, of course. And I've been back once since. But mostly I've been raking in the hours I need back in Arizona. That's a long way from Atlantic City and my family. It's been worth it, but I sure miss them."

"Do you mind if I have a second one?" The woman held the bag up. "That last one was a strawberry, and I see a yellow one in here I'd like to try. Banana, right?"

"Yes." Candy offered a reassuring smile. "And take as many as you like. Once I get back home, I'll have access to everything in the store. Not that I need the calories."

"Calories?" Mrs. Kenner laughed. "Don't know why you're fretting over that. You're as slim as they come. Now me, I'd put on five pounds a week if I worked there." She bit into the banana taffy and a childlike smile followed. "Hmm. Maybe ten. This one's good."

"Yes, it's one of my favorites, too." Candy turned her attention to the clouds outside the tiny window. From here, they looked like soft white tufts of cotton candy.

She cringed, thinking of the nickname her parents had given her as a little girl. *Cotton Candy.* Oh, how she'd disliked that name as a child. But now, all grown up and staring at the powder blue sky, she had to admit Pop was right about one thing: his familiar words, "Cotton Candy, you've got your head in the clouds again," certainly rang true. Not that she minded from this angle. No, having her head in the clouds was a good thing from her current perspective.

Her eyes grew heavy, and before long she found herself drifting off. Dreams of piloting through a storm made for an uneasy sleep. She awoke to wheels touching down and the sound of the pilot's voice. "Welcome to Newark. Looks like they got those broken clouds fixed, so we were able to land with no problem. We hope you enjoy your stay, and thank you for traveling with Eastway."

Candy groaned, then reached for her purse to touch up her lipstick.

The captain came back on for one final word to the passengers. "Folks, make sure you get all of your belongings before exiting the plane. Anything left behind will be distributed among the flight crew. Please do *not* leave your children."

Several passengers laughed aloud at that one. A family in the row in front of Candy teased their son, then laughed.

Mrs. Kenner looked over with a shrug. "His jokes are growing on me."

Candy shrugged. *No comment.* As soon as the FASTEN SEAT BELTS sign went off, she rose and stretched to get the kinks out. The line slowly moved forward toward the front of the plane. She followed along behind Mrs. Kenner, who chatted the whole way.

As they approached the front door, the same blond flight attendant greeted her with a pleasant "Have a good day." Candy nodded and looked to the woman's right. She recognized the pilot's uniform right away. Her gaze shifted to his badge. CAPTAIN DARREN FURST. The comedic pilot. He was taller than many of the pilots she'd flown with, and considerably more handsome. His dark eyes and hair distracted her for a moment, then the line of people shifted forward once again.

He gave her a polite smile, adding, "Thank you for flying with us," as she passed.

She returned the gesture with a polite nod.

"Well, there you go, honey," Mrs. Kenner whispered in her ear as they continued on their way out of the plane. "He might not be the world's best comedian, but he sure makes up for it in looks, doesn't he?"

_Please tell me he did not hear that._ Candy turned back to give him one final look. No, the captain's focus had shifted to the people behind her. Convinced he hadn't overheard them, Candy said her good-byes to Mrs. Kenner and set her sights on the great outdoors.

# two

Darren yawned and stretched, happy to be free of the confines of the cockpit. Though he loved his job, he felt cramped at times. He'd started the morning in Newark, flown to Chicago and back again. A pretty typical schedule these days, and one his seniority made possible. Others who'd worked less time with the company didn't have it so good. Many who were based in Newark didn't get to see as much of the town as they'd like, due to their hectic schedules.

" 'Night, Captain." His copilot, Larry Cason, patted him on the back as he passed by. "Get some rest."

"Mm-hmm."

Larry paused. "You got anything special planned for the Fourth of July?"

"Who, me?" Darren shrugged. "My family's all on the West Coast, remember?"

"Ah. Right." His eyes lit up. "Well, why don't you come to my place? My wife's inviting her sister, and she's single."

Darren groaned. "Remember what happened the last time you tried to fix me up with someone?"

"Yeah." Larry smiled. "I had no way of knowing Abby was so clingy. But Chelsea's not."

"Chelsea?"

"She's really sweet. Maybe a little young for you, though. She's only twenty-one."

Darren groaned. "Um, no thanks. I don't think the age gap would work."

"Hey, don't be so hard on yourself." Larry gave him a funny look. "You're not as old as you act."

"Thanks a lot."

"No, seriously." Larry scrutinized him. "You act like you're in your forties, but I know you're a lot younger. What are you, maybe thirty-two?"

"On my next birthday." Darren shrugged.

"Okay, Grandpa. Well, maybe I won't fix you up with the twenty-one-year-old, but that doesn't mean you have to curl up in a ball and pretend your dating days are behind you. What have you got to lose, anyway?" Larry's laugh rang out as he made his way off the plane. "See ya later, Gramps."

*"Gramps."* Darren groaned, then pondered Larry's words —*What have I got to lose?*—as he turned back to the cockpit to grab his belongings. As he prepared to leave the plane, someone called his name. He turned to see a familiar flight attendant. "Hey, Brooke. What's up?"

"Not much. Just wanted you to try this." She handed him a piece of candy. Saltwater taffy.

"Candy?" He gave her a curious look. "What's up with this?"

"It's taffy. Just thought you'd like a piece. One of the passengers gave me this bag." Brooke lifted up the plastic bag with a CARINI'S CONFECTIONS sticker on the side along with a picture of the boardwalk in Atlantic City.

"Good stuff." He reached for a piece. "So, taffy's a big thing in Atlantic City?"

She groaned. "How long have you worked for Eastway?"

"Four years." He spoke around the mouthful of sugary stickiness. "How come?"

"You've lived in Jersey for four years and haven't figured out that the boardwalk in Atlantic City is known for its saltwater taffy?"

"Never been to the boardwalk." He shrugged and reached for another piece and unwrapped it. "Guess I'll have to go someday."

"I'll ask Jason to plan a trip for our singles ministry," she added. "Would you go with us if we did?"

"Sure. Why not?"

"Okay. And while we're there, we'll take you to Carini's Confections. They've got the cutest little candy shop on the boardwalk."

The words *cute* and *candy* sounded pretty girlie. Still, the taffy tasted good. He couldn't argue with that.

"I'm still getting to know the Newark area," he said with a shrug. "And all of the surrounding places."

"Yeah, Jason told me you haven't even been over to Ellis Island yet. Or the Statue of Liberty."

"I know, I know. I'm just so. . ."

"Busy?"

"Yes." *And distracted. What's the point of going places if you have no one special to go there with you?*

Brooke continued chatting, and Darren tried to stay focused. However, he found himself stifling a yawn. He'd like to get home and out of this uniform. It seemed to be swallowing him up today.

"Hey, I have an idea." Brooke's eyes flashed. "Jason's picking me up. We're going to dinner at that new steak house he's been telling everyone about. Why don't you come with us?"

"You seriously want me to horn in on your date? No thanks." Though Darren valued Jason's input into his life— both as friend and singles pastor at his church—he couldn't imagine interrupting a date with the guy's fiancée. Even if the fiancée happened to be a coworker and friend.

"But there's something we want to talk to you about." Brooke pouted, then flashed a sly smile. "I've got an old friend from college I want to introduce you to."

"Oh no." He put a hand up and took a small step backward. "Not another blind date. I thought I made that plain after the last one."

"I promise it won't be like before. This one's closer to your age, and she works in D.C. In fact"—Brooke leaned in to whisper—"she's the campaign manager for Paul Cromwell.

You know who he is, right?"

"Doesn't ring a bell."

"Prominent senator from Texas, known for his conservative stance on several controversial issues. He's on FOX News all the time. And CNN, too. There are rumors Andrea's going to become his chief of staff in a few months, so we're talking big stuff here." Brooke winked. "I know how conservative you are. You two are politically perfect for each other." She jabbed Darren in the arm and he groaned.

"Oh, great. Is that how we're choosing mates now. . . according to their political stance? Is that how you and Jason fell for each other?" He put on his best newscaster voice and said, "And now, ladies and gentlemen—broadcast live from Newark, New Jersey—an interview with Brooke Antonelli and Jason Kaufman, political romanticists. They're here today to tell you the story of how they met during a nationally televised debate over opposing solutions to rising gas prices."

He shifted his gaze to Brooke, who laughed. "Actually, Jason and I have differing opinions on that," she said. "You know me. I'm a nature lover. I want to save the animals and their nature preserves. But Jason. . ." She laughed. "Well, he just wants to know why he has to pay through the nose for gas just so that the caribou can have the extra space to roam around. He says they're not going to know the difference anyway." She sighed. "He didn't take well to that SAVE THE CARIBOU sticker I put on my car."

Darren laughed. "You've got a soft heart, even when it comes to animals. That's one of the things Jason loves most about you. I know, because he told me."

"Aw."

Darren paused before adding, "Yes, but I have the opposite problem. I have yet to meet a woman with a soft heart. Most of the ones I get close to turn out to be edgy. Harsh. No soft edges at all. And a woman with political ambitions?" He shivered at the very idea. "I can only imagine. Give me a sweet woman. That's all I'm asking for. . . . Well, that and she has to have a great relationship with the Lord."

"She's out there. I know it." Brooke gave him a sympathetic look. "But don't be surprised if God brings you someone with some spunk, Darren. After all, you're as soft as a marshmallow. If you fell for someone just like yourself, where would the fun be?"

"Fun?" Darren snorted. "So, I should look for someone who is my polar opposite?"

"No, I'm just saying you don't have to have everything in common to love someone. And I'm not saying that's how you should choose a mate, per se. You ask God for His perfect will and go from there. But you'll never know if she's the one for you if you don't at least meet her. Her name is Andrea Jackson, by the way. My friend who works for the senator, I mean. She's great."

Darren groaned. "Okay, so when is this date you're setting up? And where do I take this politically-conservative-Andrea-person? Not a fancy restaurant, I hope. Someplace quick. Fast food. Then if things don't work out, I can scoot on out without hurting her feelings."

"You're such a man." Brooke rolled her eyes as she reached for her bag. "You're not taking her out for fast food. And you don't even have to go out with her at all, if you don't want to. But if you don't, you'll be missing out on an evening with a great woman. Did I mention she's a knockout, and she loves the Lord? She also does a lot of public speaking and heads up a ministry that reaches out to children in inner-city housing projects."

Okay, he had to admit. . .that last part held some appeal. Not that he minded her political leanings. They jived with his. It just seemed odd to date a woman that someone else had picked out for him. Made him feel incapable of doing it on his own.

Brooke continued, oblivious to his thoughts. "Andrea's

about as close to ideal as you're gonna get, next to me. And I'm already taken." She gave him a playful wink.

Darren followed her, his rolling bag clop-clopping behind. *Ugh.* Broken wheel. He had to remember to pick up a new bag.

And while he was at it, he'd pick up a new love life, too. The one he had right now. . . ? Well, it just didn't appear to be working.

# three

Candy walked along the boardwalk at sunset, each step drawing her closer to her family's candy store. When she caught a glimpse of the sign, her heartbeat quickened. *Thank You, Lord. Feels so good to be home.*

She entered the shop and found a handful of people lingering inside. Hmm. Not bad for an evening crowd. Then again, her older sister, Taffie, had been telling her about the family's boom in business for a while now. *Things are really hopping around here.*

From across the counter, she watched as Taffie helped a customer with his order. Caramel apples, to be precise. And a half pound of taffy. Candy could judge the weight of the bag from here. Years of working in the store had made her an expert.

She shifted her gaze to the other side of the store where Taffie's husband, Ryan, dished up chocolate ice cream—or was that Rocky Road?—and chatted a mile a minute with the customers. Nothing had changed there. He'd always been a social person, and excellent with customers. And his marketing skills had really turned things around at Carini's.

A customer pressed past her, then offered up a rushed apology. Candy nodded but didn't say a word. She didn't mind the crowd a bit. No, now that she'd returned to the place she loved most, she simply wanted to drink in the experience. To let the sweetness that hung in the air permeate her heart. To allow her mind and her somewhat overactive imagination to reel backward in time, to the many, many years she'd spent playing and working alongside her parents and sisters in this familiar place.

Oh, what sweet memories. Literally. As a youngster, she'd loved walking along the edges of the candy case, staring at the delectable goodies inside. They still wowed her. She glanced at the rows of creamy maple fudge and the tiny mounds of white divinity. Her mouth watered as she took in the rows of sticky caramel apples and the rock candy. "Mmm." She could almost taste it all from here.

And the sounds! There was still something about the joy in the customers' voices that made her grin. Who could blame them? Candy always made people happy.

*Candy always makes people happy.* Her mind tumbled backward in time again. She could almost hear Grandpa Gus's jovial voice as he teased her out of a childish sour mood. *"You have the privilege of living up to that name, honey. As much as you are able. . .make others happy. Just remember that happiness—real happiness—only comes from above, so stay tapped into the source and you'll do just fine."*

She'd done her best through the years. These days she did little to stir the waters, even when they probably needed stirring. Peaceful. That's what Mama called her. She often wondered if peaceful equaled passive.

The crowd eventually thinned and Taffie caught sight of her. She came rushing toward her with a broad smile. "You're here!"

"I'm here." Candy threw her arms around her older sister and gave her a tight squeeze. "I've missed you so much."

"Not half as much as we've missed you." Taffie rubbed her tummy and smiled. "This little one is happy to know his or her auntie Candy is sticking around this time and not high-flyin' her way to some other part of the country." Her brow wrinkled a bit as she added, "You are sticking around, aren't you?"

"If Eastway will have me." Candy shrugged. Inwardly, she wondered what might happen if she didn't get the job. Instead of dwelling on that possibility, she dove into a conversation about her upcoming interview.

About two-thirds of the way into the conversation, Ryan approached from behind the ice cream counter. He let Candy finish, then gave her a brotherly hug. "Glad you're home. How's my favorite sister-in-law?"

She gave him a pretend warning look. "Better not let Tangie hear you say that. You know how jealous she gets." Indeed, her youngest sister was very much the baby—in many respects. She thrived on being everyone's favorite.

Ryan laughed. "Well, when she returns from the glitz and glam of her off-off-Broadway show, I'll say it to her. But you're here now."

"Thanks a lot." Candy laughed. "Anyway, I'm going to wrap up the interview process in Newark tomorrow, and find an apartment there just after." She turned to her sister with a question. "Want to come apartment shopping with me? Are you feeling up to it?"

"The morning sickness ended weeks ago," Taffie said. "I'm so much better now. But before you go searching for a place to live, we have something to tell you. Or rather, something to run by you."

"You do?" Candy looked back and forth between her sister and brother-in-law. "What is it?"

Ryan gestured for her to sit at one of the small tables nearby. "I've got a cousin named Brooke who works as a flight attendant for Eastway," he explained. "She's rooming with a couple of other flight attendants at a fairly new apartment complex in Newark. She says it's a great place. Not too far from the airport, but not close enough that the planes keep you up all night."

"She's great," Taffie added. "I met her at the Antonelli family reunion a couple of months ago. I told her all about you, and she said to give you her number if the Eastway thing worked out. Told me they were going to be looking for a new roommate to share apartment costs in July. And it's July. So, what do you think?"

"Well, I think I have to think about it." Candy smiled. It certainly sounded like more than a coincidence. "So, it's in Newark. That's good."

"Yes, and I really think you'll like Brooke. She's our kind of girl." Taffie offered up a reassuring nod. "And her fiancé, Jason, is a great guy. We met him that same night. He's the singles pastor at their church in Newark. They told us all about it. Said you'd love the church. They're getting married in a few months, by the way."

"Wow." Candy thought about that a moment. "Do you go on being a singles pastor when you're married? Wouldn't that knock you right out of a job?"

"Oh, I don't know." Ryan smiled. "I led worship in our singles ministry before we got married and went on doing so after."

"Yes." Candy looked at her sister's slightly expanding midsection with a smile. "And before you know it, your baby will be grown up and ready to find his or her perfect mate."

"Bite your tongue!" Taffie laughed. "Let's don't rush things, okay?"

"Okay, okay!" She put her hands up in the air. "But you'll see what I mean. Time seems to be flying by."

They all grew quiet for a moment. Ryan finally broke the silence. "I can tell you one thing. I'll probably go on leading worship when the baby's that age. In fact, I might just go on singing and praising God till I'm a grandpa. You know me."

"Yeah, I know you." Candy nodded. Ryan had such a heart for singles. The candy shop stayed filled year round with young adults, especially now that they offered specialty coffees and Christian karaoke night.

Before long they were caught up in conversation about the good old days. Candy laughed through several of the stories, particularly the ones that focused on her middle-child syndrome.

"I'm over that now," she assured Taffie. "I promise. I'm not the insecure little girl I once was. Something about flying helped me overcome all of that."

"So, you're okay with being stuck in the middle?" Taffie teased.

"I can think of worse places," Candy said. "So, yes. I'm okay with being stuck in the middle."

Funny, sitting here in the candy shop, she felt completely comfortable. She just had to wonder if she would go on feeling this comfortable once she faced the fine folks at Eastway Airlines.

❧

Darren rambled through the empty rooms of his house, wondering what it would feel like to actually have people in those rooms. In the two years since he'd splurged and purchased the home in Bridgewater, he'd had a few friends over. Even hosted a barbecue on the deck. But what he longed for—ached for, really—was a wife and children. People he could love who would love him in return. He wanted to fill the house with laughter and music. Anything other than the weighty silence or the occasional hum of the dishwasher.

He wanted the very thing he'd also longed for as a child, but never really had. A normal family. With an overbearing mother and a passive father, he'd missed out as a kid. It wasn't asking too much to see some degree of normalcy now, was it?

Oh, he wouldn't come out and admit his desire for the married life to his friends and coworkers. Why do that, when he'd managed to convince them he hoped to stay single forever? Yes, he'd done a fine job of making them believe he loved his current situation. If only he could convince himself.

He walked through the living room, stopping at the large empty aquarium. Maybe one day he'd actually buy a fish. In the meantime he had all the goods. Castle. Rocks. Food. You name it.

*Someday.*

Darren walked through the large kitchen to the back door. Sliding it open, he stepped out onto the wooden deck—a deck he'd built with his own hands. Off in the distance, the three oak trees he'd planted last summer were finally starting to look like something more than scraggly twigs. Hopefully in a few years they'd stand tall and sturdy.

Through the crack in the door, he heard his cell phone ringing in the house and scrambled to catch it before it went to voice mail. He'd been secretly longing for the call from Brooke about her friend Andrea. Unfortunately, the voice on the other end of the line was decidedly male.

"Darren?"

He recognized his friend Gary's voice right off and responded, "Hey, what's up?"

Gary's next words totally threw him. "I got a written warning, man. Eastway's doing everything they can to get rid of me."

"Wait. . .are you serious?"

"Yes. But this time I've got the union on my side. And we're pretty sure we know what's really happening here. Eastway is dropping employees right and left because of the increase in fuel prices. They're just using my warnings from last month as an excuse. No one's job is safe." Gary went on and on, anger lacing his words. Darren tried not to let his friend's emotions spill over on him, but he found it difficult. *"No one's job is safe"?*

"But it doesn't make sense," he said. "You've got seniority. You've been with the company two and a half years." Sure, Gary had received a verbal warning, and then a write-up. . . all related to his volatile temper and attitude with the crew several weeks prior. But he seemed to be doing better, of late. Why would they let him go now?

"Two and a half years isn't long enough, apparently," Gary said. "Rumor has it anyone who's flown for Eastway for less than three could be asked to go."

"Something about this just doesn't sound right." Darren raked his fingers through his hair, growing more frustrated by the moment. "I heard Eastway just hired a couple of new pilots this past week. Why would they yank your job away and give it to someone else?"

"One word. Females."

"W–what?"

"They're trying to meet their quota of women. I'm guessing Eastway has to keep a certain ratio of male-female pilots. Somehow they got off-kilter. I'd be willing to bet those new hires were women. So, decide for yourself."

"That's the most absurd thing I've ever heard." Darren began to pace, trying to make sense of this. "Quotas are a thing of the past. And the union would never stand for it. So, if there's even a hint of sexism, they're going to get to the bottom of this."

"I'm counting on it. But even if they skirt the issue—pun intended—Eastway still won't be in good shape. Not with fuel prices so high."

Fuel prices were high, sure. Airlines everywhere were cutting back. Some had even started charging for baggage. And meal services were almost nonexistent, especially for regional carriers like Eastway. But. . .letting pilots go? Something about that just wasn't right.

He finally voiced the inevitable question. "So, do you think I'm next?"

"You?" Gary laughed. "You've been with Eastway longer than most of us. What's it been? Four years?"

"Four and a half."

"Right. And your record is clean as a whistle. I wouldn't imagine you'll be going anywhere."

Darren breathed a sigh of relief but knew he couldn't celebrate just yet. Nor would he want to, with his friend facing a job loss. No, what he really wanted to do was head up to the Eastway offices and give the higher-ups a piece of his mind.

He wouldn't, of course. It wasn't in his nature. What was it Brooke had said, again? Ah yes. *"You're soft as a marshmallow."*

*Soft as a marshmallow.*

As the frustration took hold, Darren wished—just this once—he had the courage to toss his marshmallow mentality right out the window.

# four

Just one week after arriving home in New Jersey, Candy moved into the crowded two-bedroom apartment in Newark with Brooke Antonelli and two other Eastway flight attendants. She loved her new place almost as much as she loved her new roomies. Brooke, Lilly, and Shawneda each surprised her with their uniqueness and their outgoing personalities. In some ways it felt like being with her sisters again.

She'd no sooner dropped her final load of boxes in the front hall than Lilly grabbed her hand. "You're going to be sharing a room with me. Hope you're okay with all the colors. I love color."

Candy followed along behind the petite Asian beauty until they entered the bedroom to the right of the living area. She'd seen the space a few days earlier, of course, but was still amazed at the effort that had gone into decorating it. The bright orange walls took her breath away. Literally. "You—you've done a great job in here."

"Are you okay with the bedding? It's a little bright."

"I love it." She looked at the orange and teal comforter and smiled. No, it wasn't what she would've picked out for herself, but why not expand her horizons? *My life could use a little color.*

"Good thing we already had the extra twin bed, right?" Lilly grinned. "My last roomie—Reagan—went to work for Continental. She's in Houston permanently now."

"Right. A friend of mine from Arizona just went to work for them."

"Male or female?" Lilly asked.

"Male." Candy smiled as she thought about Russ, her old

28

flying buddy. Her smile was followed by a few moments of reflective thought. Seemed like all the pilots she knew eventually parted ways. . .each heading off to his or her own airline. Were there any long-lasting relationships in this business?

"Did I hear someone talking about men?" Shawneda, the oldest of the roommates, entered the room and plopped down on Lilly's bed, making herself at home.

"Oh, we were just talking about a friend of Candy's," Lilly said.

"Boyfriend?" Shawneda's brows elevated slightly. "Tell me everything. Don't leave out even one teensy-tiny detail." She stared up at Candy, apparently ready for a lengthy romantic tale.

"No, you don't understand." Candy shook her head. "I'm not dating anyone right now. I was just talking about an old friend of mine who's based out of Houston now."

"Houston!" The tone of Shawneda's voice changed. "Girl, I'm from Texas. Maybe you could tell from my accent." She went into a descriptive story about life in the South, and had the other girls laughing within minutes. All questions about Candy's love life faded to the background.

The doorbell rang, interrupting Shawneda's dramatic story about a horse-riding adventure she'd gone on when she was sixteen. All of the girls looked at the door with surprised expressions on their faces.

"Were you expecting anyone?" Lilly asked.

"Not me," Candy said. "No one even knows I'm living here yet. . .except my family. And they're in A.C."

"A.C.?" Shawneda's puzzled expression almost made Candy laugh.

"Atlantic City." Lilly rolled her eyes. "Seriously, Shawneda. You're not in Texas anymore."

"I know, I know." The bell rang again. "I didn't invite anyone over," Shawneda said. "I'm not in a company frame of mind tonight. Too tired. Just give me a bubble bath and a good book."

"Me, too." Lilly shrugged.

"Maybe Brooke will get it," Shawneda said with a yawn.

Seconds later, Candy heard voices at the front door. Male voices. She followed along behind Shawneda and Lilly.

Brooke stood in the open doorway, squealing as two handsome guys entered.

The taller one reached to sweep Brooke into his arms. "Sorry I'm so early. But I was anxious to see you."

Candy watched this interaction with a smile. *Aha. This must be the fiancé.*

As if to answer her question, Shawneda said, "Oh, it's just Jason." With a wave of her hand, she headed to the kitchen.

"I heard that, Shawneda!" Jason called out. "I love you, too."

"Yeah, yeah. . ." Her voice trailed off as she disappeared into the other room.

Candy shifted her attention to the other man. . .the one standing next to Jason. He looked a little uncomfortable. She tried not to stare, but something about him felt familiar. Tall. . .about five eleven. Dark wavy hair. Deep blue eyes. Nice build. Hmm. *Where have I seen this guy before?*

His taste in wardrobe was nice—button-up shirt with tie. Great slacks. All in all, he was very well put together. He glanced her way and nodded, his blue eyes gazing into hers.

"It's going to take me a few minutes to get ready," Brooke said. "Do you guys mind just making yourselves at home?" She turned her gaze to Candy and Lilly. "Would you mind keeping them entertained? Please. I won't be long."

"Oh, I, um. . ." Candy tried not to stumble over her words, though she felt a little put-on-the-spot. "I–I'm Candy."

"Jason." The fiancé extended his hand. "And this is my best friend, Darren Furst."

"Aha!" She snapped her fingers as the realization set in. "You're a pilot."

"I am." A smile lit his face and she took note of two strategically placed dimples. Very nice. *His flight comedy might not be great, but he's got a winning smile.*

"You work for Eastway."

"Yes." He gave a hint of a smile. "How did you know that?"

She did her best acting job as she said, "Good afternoon, ladies and gentlemen. Welcome aboard Eastway Airlines flight so-and-so from Chicago to Newark. This is your captain, Darren Furst. Not second, first."

Lilly laughed. "Sounds just like him!"

Darren groaned and slapped himself on the forehead. "I don't know if I should be flattered or offended. I can't believe you actually remembered that."

"Well, I'm—" She never got to finish because Shawneda reentered the room with sodas in hand. She passed them off to the guys and before long a conversation ensued.

Candy spent the next few minutes taking in Darren. In person—dressed in street clothes—he looked like a regular guy. Nothing pretentious about him. And, as they talked about the singles ministry at the church, his love for the Lord came shining through. In fact, it was evident in both his conversation and his kind manner.

So, what had ruffled her feathers that day on the plane? Had she really judged him based only on his voice? Or was it her bias against male pilots, in general, that prompted such a knee-jerk reaction. *Ouch. Can't believe I really admitted to that. I have an issue with male pilots?*

She'd tucked the idea away for months, but—being honest with herself—she'd struggled with the way the guys in flight school treated her. And she'd suffered more than her share of jokes as a skydiving pilot, too. The male pilots didn't always treat her with the respect she deserved, but she'd pushed their comments aside and moved forward. Was her knee-jerk reaction to Darren on the plane last week rooted in something deeper, perhaps?

Candy knew the statistics, knew what she was up against in this industry. She already had several things working against her. . .age, for one. Most new hires were twenty-seven to forty-two, and she'd just turned twenty-three. Many had more flight hours. Still, she felt she had what it took to be competitive. And she certainly knew what it meant to be patient.

"Are we all best friends now?"

Candy looked up as she heard Brooke's happy-go-lucky voice ring out. "S—sure."

"Well, that's great." Her new friend flashed a winning smile, then checked her appearance in the mirror on the wall. " 'Cause I want you to come to dinner with us."

"Come with you?" Candy shook her head, stunned by the idea. "But. . .I can't."

"Of course you can." Brooke sat next to her on the sofa. "We're all friends here. And we all work for the same company." Gazing lovingly at Jason, she added, "Well, all but Handsome here."

"Sure, come with us," Jason said. "It'll be great."

Candy sought out Darren's eyes, to see his reaction. She saw nothing but friendliness and encouragement there.

"I—I guess," she said finally. "Just let me change my blouse. I'm not dressed to go out."

"We'll wait," Brooke said. "Just hurry, okay? I'm starved."

As she changed into her favorite pink blouse and capris, Candy thought about Darren. He had that boy-next-door look about him. Shame washed over her as she realized how she'd judged him before even getting to know him.

"Sorry about that, Lord," she whispered. "I'm gonna keep an eye on that from now on."

While she was at it, she might just keep an eye on the handsome pilot, too.

❧

Darren did his best to pay attention as Brooke went on and on about her upcoming wedding plans. However, his thoughts kept shifting to the young woman to his right. She must be a new flight attendant. He'd have to ask Jason later. But Brooke's words, "We all work for the same company," left little other meaning. Still, she didn't have that same bubbly personality that so many of the flight attendants had. There was a quietness about her, almost a reserved nature.

At a break in the conversation, he turned to her. "So, you're Candy." When she nodded, he said, "I don't think I ever heard your last name."

"Candy Carini," Brooke explained. "Remember? I told you all about Carini's Confections on the boardwalk in Atlantic City? They're famous."

"Well, not exactly famous. Though I can say my parents had the right idea by making sure they put God at the center of their careers, no matter the obstacles." Candy's cheeks turned a pretty shade of pink and she shrugged. "We've been in business a long time. We have longevity on our side. And now we're finally on the Internet. That helps."

At once his thoughts sailed back to the saltwater taffy Brooke had given him on the plane. "Oh, right. I remember now. You gave some candy to Brooke on a flight a week or so ago."

"Yes, that's right." After a moment's pause, she added, "Isn't it funny how the Lord works? I didn't know either of you back then. Now I'm rooming with Brooke and we're all fellow employees." Another smile lit her already-beautiful face and caused her eyes to sparkle. "I just got hired on."

He wanted to ask for more details, but the waitress appeared with their food. By the time they'd been served, his thoughts shifted back to the candy shop. "So, tell me about this name of yours. Candy from the candy shop?"

He watched with a hint of a smile as she sighed. "Yeah. My parents are funny like that. And trust me, I've heard every joke in the book, so you might as well save yourself the time and trouble."

"Taffie says they call you Cotton Candy." Brooke gave her a teasing look.

"Um, yeah. And thanks for bringing it up." Candy's cheeks turned a deep crimson. "I'll never live that down."

"Well, I won't be making fun of your name or anyone else's." Darren gazed into her dark brown eyes and offered a sympathetic look. "If anyone knows what it feels like to have a name that people make fun of, I do."

"True, true." She grinned. "Furst, not second." After a brief chuckle, she asked, "So, where are you from? And where did you train?"

"Oh, I'm from Southern California. Went to San Diego Flight Training School. Pretty well known."

"Sure." Candy's eyes lit with recognition, making her all the more beautiful. "I've heard a lot about them. Do you know about Double Eagle Aviation in Tucson?"

"Sure." He nodded. "One of the pilots I flew with last week got her wings at Double Eagle about six years ago."

"Her? It was a woman?" Candy smiled.

"Yeah." He shrugged. After his recent conversation with Gary, it might not be the best idea to get into a lengthy chat about women in the industry, particularly female pilots. Not that Candy would mind, most likely. Most of the flight attendants didn't really care if their pilots were male or female, as long as they kept the plane in the air when it was supposed to be in the air.

"Women are making inroads at the airlines," he said, and then shrugged. *I'll just leave it at that.*

"Hey, don't get Darren started on women." Jason laughed. "I think he's just sensitive. We've been trying to find Mrs. Right for him for ages now, and so far it's been a no go in every situation."

Darren shrugged. "I just don't see the purpose in dating. Maybe I have a different view of things. I guess I'm a little old-fashioned."

"Not at all." Candy looked at him and shrugged. "I think dating is a waste of time, too. It's almost like you're trying people out, one at a time. Seems kind of. . .odd."

Brooke giggled. "It's funny, hearing Darren talk about women at the dinner table. Usually it's the other way around with pilots. When they're flying they talk about women, and when they're with a woman, they talk about flying."

Jason laughed long and loud at that one. Darren felt the tips of his ears heat up, something he could never seem to control when embarrassed. He'd have to talk to Jason later about making him the brunt of every joke, especially in front of someone as pretty as Candy.

Brooke changed the direction of the conversation at that very moment. He breathed a sigh of relief as she started talking about a passenger on a recent flight, one who'd given her fits over a spilled soft drink.

Though he tried to pay attention, he found his gaze shifting back to Candy. The name suited her. She was sweet, through and through.

Hmm. Sweet. What was it he'd said to Brooke that day on the plane? *"Give me a sweet woman. That's all I'm asking for."*

Maybe. . .just maybe. . .the Lord had dropped one in his lap.

## five

Candy spent her first days at Eastway training on crew resource management and learning everything humanly possible about the aircraft. This gave her some time to get adjusted to the idea that she now belonged to a family. . .a very large family with eclectic brothers and sisters.

Not that she minded. No, being grafted into this new and strange place felt like an adventure. And she couldn't balk at the idea of a solid paycheck. Sure, there would be school loans to pay off in a couple of years, but she didn't have to fret over them just yet. By the time they came due, she'd be earning higher pay, anyway.

On Tuesday, after a particularly long day, Candy found herself walking through the Eastway terminal, waiting on Brooke's flight to arrive. They'd agreed to meet at the gate and then ride home together. Knowing she had over twenty minutes to kill, Candy stopped at a gift shop and purchased a soft drink, then strolled the long hallway near the gate, looking at the photographs on the wall. She'd seen them in passing a couple of times before but never paused long enough to actually take them in.

Candy stopped and looked at a photograph of Amelia Earhart, then read the information underneath. THE NINETY-NINES IS AN ORGANIZATION OF FEMALE PILOTS FOUNDED IN 1929 BY 99 LICENSED WOMEN PILOTS.

"The Ninety-Nines." *Lord, thanks for the reminder.* Many of her friends in Tucson had joined when they got their wings. She'd put it off, promising herself she would make it a priority as soon as she got her first gig with a real airline. *And now I can join.*

Candy couldn't hide the smile, as she looked at the next photo of a female pilot from the 1940s. The text under the photo inspired her. OVER 5,000 LICENSED FEMALE PILOTS FROM THIRTY-SIX COUNTRIES HOLD MEMBERSHIP IN THE NINETY-NINES. *Wow.* A shiver ran down her spine. *And soon I'll be one of them.*

One by one, she read about the inroads females had made in the industry. By the time she reached the last photograph, Candy convinced herself she not only needed to join the Ninety-Nines, she should link arms with other female pilots in the area to do something special. Maybe a banquet of some sort. They could invite someone of notoriety to speak. *Hmm. I'll have to think on that.*

Candy glanced at her watch. Brooke's flight still wasn't due in for another eleven minutes. She turned her attention to the wall on the opposite side of the hallway. The faces of several Eastway pilots greeted her, their smiles broad and inviting.

*Soon. . .my picture will hang here, too.*

She made her way down the line, taking them all in. One after the other, they held her interest. Sure, most were men. She figured that. But, when she reached the end of the row, she realized she'd seen photos of only three female pilots in the bunch. What was up with that? Looked like the percentage was lower than she'd thought. An uneasy feeling gripped her as she thought it through. Just as quickly, she released that feeling to the Lord.

*You gave me this job. I know I can trust You with it.*

Candy paused when she reached the photo of a familiar handsome pilot. Captain Darren Furst. She stared at his features for some time. A passenger rushed by and bumped up against her. "Sorry about that!" he called out as he sprinted toward the gate.

"No problem." She turned back to face Darren's photo, examining him from his dark wavy hair down to his broad shoulders. His bright blues eyes caught her attention, as always. Her father always said you could tell a lot about a person by looking into his eyes. She gave them another look. Yep. Warm and inviting. And his smile was genuine.

"A penny for your thoughts."

Candy turned around as she heard Brooke's voice. "H–hey. You're early."

"Mm-hmm. Whatcha lookin' at?" Brooke's eyebrows elevated mischievously.

"Oh. . ." Candy gestured down the wall, trying to look nonchalant. "Just trying to get to know my fellow pilots. I've met a few of them in person."

"Like this handsome fellow." Brooke pointed at Darren's picture, and Candy did her best to look sufficiently disinterested.

"Oh, Darren? He's worked for Eastway longer than most. Interesting."

"He's the best." Brooke took her by the arm, then whispered, "I've known him for ages, and he's really the cream on top of the coffee. Unlike some of the others. But then, you're going to give them all a run for their money."

"What?"

"Nothing." Brooke gave her a wink. "I'm just saying that you're going to be every bit as awesome. And that's a good thing."

"This isn't a competition, Brooke." Candy turned to face her. "And I sure don't want it to turn into one. Things are hard enough for female pilots as it is, without any comparisons."

"Oh, I know. I'm not saying that. And I love Darren. He's the best. I'm just glad Eastway came to their senses and hired on a few more women. Things were pretty out of balance before, that's all." She flashed a bright smile. "Let's get out of here, okay? I'm starving."

"Me, too." Candy nodded. "I skipped lunch today."

"Shawneda's cooking. She's making Texas barbecue. Brisket, to be precise. And I think she said something about

Southwestern beans and some sort of potatoes. Are you game?"

"Sounds great."

As they left the hallway, Candy's gaze shifted back to Darren's photo one last time. She felt a little foolish, like a child with her hand caught in the cookie jar.

Oh well. She'd come to Newark to fly planes, not fall for handsome pilots. There would be plenty of time to think of her love life later. Right now she had bigger fish to fry.

ھ

On Tuesday evening Darren ended a long day of flying and made the drive home, completely exhausted. He'd barely made it through the door when his cell phone rang. Determined to get out of his uniform before dealing with anything important, he made the decision to return the call after he'd had a bite to eat.

After changing clothes and fixing a sandwich, he finally reached for the phone, ready to return the call. When he saw Jason's number, Darren relaxed. Thank goodness. Nothing work related. He punched the SEND key, leaning back against the sofa with the sandwich in hand.

"Well, hey there." Jason laughed. "Thought maybe you were avoiding me. Did you listen to my message?"

"Message? No, sorry. Didn't even realize you'd left one. I just saw that you'd called." He went on to explain his exhaustion and his long day.

"Ah, okay. Well, Brooke put me up to this. You remember that friend of hers she told you about—the one who works for the senator?"

Darren perked up right away. "Andrea." He took a bite of the sandwich and listened to his friend's words.

"Yes, she's going to be in town for a speaking engagement. Brooke told her you might be interested in going out for coffee. Nothing stressful."

"Ah." Darren wiped a bit of mustard off his lip and took another bite of the sandwich.

"So, what about it? Saturday afternoon at four? That way she has plenty of time to get back to the hotel to prepare for her speaking gig. And look at it this way, if things don't work out, she won't be sticking around for any length of time."

"Right." It might be a safe plan. Not that he was hoping things would go wrong. He really didn't know what to think, to be quite honest. After another bite of sandwich and a few concerned thoughts, Darren shifted gears. He wanted to be polite. . .to stay focused on Andrea, but his thoughts kept shifting back to the beautiful woman he'd met a few nights before. Candy Carini.

"Can I ask you a few questions about Brooke's roommate?" he finally worked up the courage to ask.

"Which one?" Jason laughed. "Every other week there's a new one."

"The latest one." *The gorgeous brunette with those amazing eyes.* After a moment's pause, he added, "I'm so torn over this. You know my policy. I never date any of the flight attendants. Never."

"Flight attendants?" Jason sounded confused. "Wait. Who are we talking about here? Lilly or Shawneda?"

"Neither. I'm talking about Candy Carini."

"Darren, I—um—hate to be the one to tell you this, but Candy's not a flight attendant."

"Of course she is. I heard her say she just got hired on."

"Yes, she did. She's an Eastway employee, for sure. But she's not a flight attendant. She's a—"

Darren's stomach plummeted as he finished his friend's sentence. "She's a pilot?"

"Yes." Jason exhaled loudly. "Did you miss the part where she asked you where you got your wings? And that whole thing about the flight school in Tucson. She was telling you her own story, dude. You should've been reading between the lines."

Darren felt like slapping himself in the head. *How did I miss that?* "Did I say anything embarrassing about female pilots?" He squeezed his eyes shut. "Tell me I didn't."

"Nah. There was something about women making inroads in the industry, or something like that. But nothing negative. Why?" Jason appeared to hesitate before asking, "You got a problem with women pilots?"

"No. . .not really."

" 'Not really'?"

Darren sighed. "A couple of friends just lost their jobs, and I heard they were being replaced by new hires. Females." He went on to explain his mixed feelings. "Just seems pointless to let someone go because of their sex. Ya know?"

"Yeah," Jason agreed. "But I'd be willing to bet it has nothing to do with that. Brooke says this girl is really good. And she's thrilled to be flying for Eastway. So, go easy on her, okay?"

"Of course. Oh, and by the way. . ."

"Yeah?"

"You forgot to give me Andrea's number." Darren reached for a pen, ready to think of someone other than Candy Carini.

When he hung up from his call with Jason, Darren paced the room, a number of thoughts rolling through his head. *Candy is a pilot. A pilot.* That changed everything. Not that he had any intention of asking her out. Not at all. But, to even befriend a female pilot. . .in light of the current conditions? What would Gary say? Or the others, for that matter. No, he'd better tuck that idea right back into his flight bag and forget about it.

On the other hand, Candy was new to Eastway and would need friends. He couldn't very well avoid her just to save face, could he? And besides, she was a believer. God wouldn't think very highly of Darren if he deliberately opted out of a friendship because of the other guys.

Determined to shift his focus, Darren finally worked up the courage to call the politically perfect Andrea to confirm their coffee date. He felt like a traitor as he punched in her number. Hadn't he just told Candy over dinner that he didn't think much of dating? And here he was, calling up a stranger to ask her out.

*I'm just doing this for Jason and Brooke. One date and I'll probably never see Andrea again.*

She answered on the third ring. Andrea had a strong, confident voice. . .so strong that it took him by surprise. She jumped on the idea of the coffee date, adding that her schedule was tight. "I hope you're okay with a getting-to-know-you pre-date," she said. "Kind of gets the awkwardness out of the way."

*Getting-to-know-you pre-date?* He groaned internally. From the businesslike sound in her voice, she'd probably record every detail of the evening on a spreadsheet. Or worse. Come with a prepared speech on men and politics. *Stop it, Darren. You don't know anything about her.*

By the time they ended the call, she'd won him over with her wit and her verbal speed. *Man, this girl can talk a mile a minute.* Not that he minded. No, having someone else do the talking saved him from having to do it.

Now, if only she could save him from having to actually meet her for coffee. . .that would be a trick.

# six

On Saturday afternoon Darren arrived at the coffee shop with his stomach in knots. What was it about first dates—especially blind dates—that made him feel like a kid all over again?

He looked around the room, thankful to see Andrea hadn't yet arrived. He knew what she'd be wearing—a navy blue jacket and slacks with a white blouse. She'd been very specific about that. For once, he was happy to be early. It would give him time to collect his thoughts while waiting.

Darren took a seat at a table and continued the silent prayer session he'd begun in the car. *Lord, You know my heart. And You know how awkward this is for me. Just please guide me. And, Lord, if the woman I'm supposed to marry comes walking through that door, then I give You permission to do whatever You like to let me know. It's gonna take something pretty big, though, 'cause I'm not convinced I'm supposed to be here at all.*

Minutes later, a petite redhead entered the store. Her hair, straight and squared off at the shoulders, gave her a professional appearance, sure. But the rest of her? Wow. Not what he'd been expecting at all. Her small physique caught him by surprise. Darren had imagined a political powerhouse to be tall and sturdy. Sort of a broad-shouldered woman. This one looked more like someone's kid sister. Dimples and all. Her shiny red hair looked just right against the pale complexion and splattering of freckles.

Okay, now what? He'd prepared himself to be disinterested. But so many things about this woman struck him as interesting.

"Darren Furst?" When he nodded, she extended her hand.

"I'm Andrea. Great to meet you."

"You, too."

He rose and pulled out a chair. She sat and placed her briefcase on the table. He half expected her to open it and begin a business meeting. Her gaze followed his to the bag. "Oh, sorry about that. But it's leather and I hate to put it on the ground."

"Oh, trust me, I understand," he said, once again taking his seat. "So, um. . ." He felt his nerves kick in and steadied his breathing. "Brooke tells me you're Paul Cromwell's campaign manager."

"That's right." Her face lit up. "Great man, and a great leader. Very well loved in Texas."

"How long has he been in office?"

"He came to D.C. in '92." She maintained her joyous expression as she talked about him. "And he's a well-respected senator. People on both sides of the fence love working with him."

"Wow."

"Yes. And I know we've just elected a new president, but it's not too soon to be thinking ahead. We're looking forward to the next presidential campaign," she explained. "And early polls have shown us that Senator Cromwell is a viable candidate to run for office. He's a great guy, and I know he'd be perfect for the job. He's truly one of the godliest men I've ever known, and his wife is amazing, as well. Perfect first couple. But we've got a long road ahead of us."

At this point, Darren had to wonder if Andrea had time for a relationship. Sounded like she was up to her eyeballs in work.

Still, there was something special about her. He sensed her passion, sure, but it was more than that. As she began to talk about the issues that affected their country, he saw her heart for the Lord shining through.

Eventually her conversation slowed, and Andrea pulled

a slip of paper out of her briefcase. She showed him some things she'd jotted down. "I know this sounds crazy, but I've learned to just get this part over with. It's my getting-to-know-you list."

"What?" He glanced at it, intrigued. "Wow. I have to answer all of those questions?"

"Only if you want to." She laughed. "But trust me, it helps to get some of the big stuff out of the way first. So, if you're game, I'm game. I'll answer if you will."

"Sure. I guess so."

He spent the next few minutes answering her preliminary questions. "I grew up in California. I have never been married. My last relationship ended amicably. I've piloted for Eastway for four years. I'm hoping to find someone with an amazing work ethic who shares my love of God, church, contemporary worship music, and Christian concerts. And I like quiet walks on the beach."

*I like walks on the beach? Where in the world did that come from?*

Darren could've slapped himself. He'd only been to the beach three or four times since moving to New Jersey.

Andrea clicked off her answers to the same questions in short order: "I'm the oldest of four children. Raised in the D.C. area. Top of my graduating class, both in high school and at Stanford. Just out of college, I served as an aid to a prominent senator. Dated loosely but never had time for a serious relationship. No pets. Don't have time or energy. Love the Lord. Believe firmly in placing Him at the center of every relationship."

Darren gave the same one-word answer he'd used earlier: "Wow." For whatever reason, he couldn't think of anything else to say.

≈

"C'mon, Candy. We won't stay long. Just come with us."

Candy looked up into Lilly's pouting eyes as she answered.

"I have a flight tomorrow. My first. I can't stay out late."

"Late? It's not even five o'clock yet. And I'm just talking about coffee here, not dinner. You'll be back before the sun goes down. But come with us, please. We're bored."

As they made the drive, Shawneda carried on about a male flight attendant who'd caught her eye.

"You're thinking of dating a fellow employee?" Candy quirked a brow. "I thought most airlines advised against that."

Shawneda shrugged. "Not Eastway. As long as it doesn't interfere with my work in any way, I'm free to date who I like."

"Wow." Candy shook her head. "Well, you can count me out of that one."

"Listen to her." Lilly giggled. "She's probably got an old boyfriend back in Tucson that she's not telling us about. Someone other than that Russ guy, I mean. That's why she's got her antennae down. A handsome guy could walk right by her and she wouldn't even notice."

"Oh, I'd notice." Candy forced herself not to think about Darren's gorgeous blue eyes. "But I'd look the other way. Right now God has given me a chance to have the job of my dreams, and I'm not going to do anything to blow it."

"So you're telling me. . .even if He brought Mr. Right and plopped him down right in front of you, you'd look the other way."

"Right now, yes." Candy nodded. "I wouldn't have any choice. And if he was truly God's man for me, he'd realize the timing wasn't right. Not yet, anyway. I've got to get through this transition I'm in before I could even think about a man." Should she tell them that she'd tried to balance work and relationships before, and it had never ended well? Maybe not.

Thankfully, Lilly dove into an animated story about a boy she used to date when she was in her teens. Shawneda countered with a harrowing tale of a relationship gone wrong when she worked at a pizza parlor during college. She'd just reached the crux of the story when they arrived at the coffee shop. They entered the crowded room, the scent of the coffee drawing them in.

Shawneda stopped her pizza story midstream just inside the door. "Whoa."

"What?" Candy followed her gaze. "Oh, wow." Darren Furst. With a woman. A really pretty woman. Polished and professional in appearance, the woman put her in mind of a talk-show host, or something along those lines. Was she a coworker, perhaps? She sure didn't look like a pilot. Not that pilots had a particular look.

"Oh, man. I know that girl," Shawneda whispered after examining her from a distance. "High-powered political type. Andrea something-or-other. Brooke introduced me to her a couple months ago. She lives in DC."

"So, do we go over and say hello?" Lilly turned to head that way, but Candy grabbed her by the arm.

"No. It looks like they're on a date. Leave them alone." The last thing she wanted to do was interrupt someone's private time.

"A date?" Shawneda and Lilly practically squealed in unison.

Lowering her voice, Lilly echoed, "A date? From what I hear, he's too career focused."

Shawneda shook her head. "Personally, I think some woman must've broken his heart. Never made any sense to me that he didn't get out more and date. If I were five or six years older, I'd slip my arm through his and march him down the aisle." She giggled, but Candy could see a serious look in her eye.

"He told me he wasn't keen on dating, but it sure looks like he's getting out now." Candy grabbed a package of coffee to hide from Darren as he looked their way. *So much for all that stuff he said. Old-fashioned, huh?*

Lilly nudged her. "You're buying a bag of coffee to take

back to the apartment?"

"Um, no. Yeah. Maybe." She peeked around the edge of the bag, trying to get a look at Andrea. She was pretty, no doubt. But was she Darren's type?

*Darren's type? Where did that come from?*

They inched their way up in line, the girls going on and on about Darren's sad dating life. . .or lack thereof, as Lilly put it. Candy refused to join in. He could date whomever he wanted. What business was it of hers?

"That Darren is a marshmallow," Shawneda said with a sigh. "I can't see him paired up with a dynamo like that."

"Oh?" Candy looked her way, curious.

"Yeah. She could steamroll right over him. Brooke told me she's a real powerhouse. She's been interviewed on nearly every major news station, and the *New York Times* ran a piece on her a few months ago. We're talking about a major player here. In political arenas, I mean."

"Not Darren's type at all." Lilly wrinkled her nose as they stepped forward in line. "I always pictured him with a schoolteacher. Or a librarian maybe."

"A librarian?" Shawneda snorted. "He needs someone with a lot of pizzazz to bring him out of his shell. Like, maybe a cruise ship singer or a Hollywood starlet."

Candy could hardly keep her thoughts to herself after such a ridiculous comment. Darren was an easygoing, friendly soul, someone who just needed a secure, steady woman at his side. "I see him with a business woman of some sort. Confident, but not outlandish."

"Why not a deep-sea diver or a brain surgeon?" A familiar male voice rang out from behind them. *Darren.* Candy felt her cheeks heat up. She didn't turn around. She didn't dare.

"Then again," he continued, "my aunt Lucy always said I'd be a pastor and would marry the church pianist. So I guess all of the females in my life have missed the mark when it comes to my dating life."

Shawneda and Lilly turned to face him, giggling like schoolgirls.

"Don't you know better than to sneak up on a girl when she's talking about a handsome man?" Shawneda crooned.

Candy cringed, thankful to suddenly be at the front of the line. She quickly ordered a cup of coffee, then paid for it, wishing she could somehow escape Darren's gaze. Still, she couldn't avoid him forever. She turned his way as Shawneda placed her order.

"I'm sorry about that. I'm usually not so free with my opinions. And I've never been accused of being a gossip before. Don't know what came over me." She tried to take a sip of her coffee, but it burned her lip. *Ouch.*

"Oh, I know what came over you." He gestured toward the other women. "I have it on good authority a lot of chatter about male-female relationships goes on in that apartment of yours."

"Hey now." Shawneda gave him a warning look. "We're not that bad."

"We're not that *good*, either," Lilly whispered, then laughed.

"Brooke says you're expert matchmakers," Darren added. "I think she credited Lilly for matching her up with Jason, even."

"That's right." Lilly grinned. "My doing. All my doing."

"Well, you and God." Shawneda jabbed her with an elbow. "But it's true, we're expert matchmakers. For everyone but ourselves."

"It's all harmless fun," Lilly said, as she stepped up to the counter to order her drink. "None of us has found the perfect man yet, anyway. Except Brooke, I mean."

Candy sighed. It might've been harmless fun, but Darren had overheard and possibly taken offense. Surely he didn't take well to being talked about behind his back. His dating life—or lack thereof—was none of their business.

The embarrassment that had taken hold of Candy just

moments before was now replaced with shame. *Lord, I'm sorry. I try so hard to guard my tongue, and look what I've done this time.*

Darren reached the counter and ordered two coffees, then promptly returned to the cute little redhead. She talked a mile a minute, capturing his attention. Candy nudged the other girls toward the opposite side of the coffee shop. She'd suffered enough embarrassment for one night, thank you very much. No point in carrying things one bit further.

Still, as they took their seats, her gaze kept shifting back to Darren. She'd been right about one thing. He needed a confident woman at his side. Problem was, the woman in the seat next to his appeared almost too confident. More the steamroller sort. Darren was hardly getting a word in edgewise.

Then again, maybe he liked that. Some guys did.

*Why am I even thinking about what Darren Furst likes and doesn't like?* Candy shook her head and sighed, then shifted her focus back to Shawneda and Lilly. This quirky pair certainly gave her enough to think about, anyway.

❧

As his getting-to-know-you date with Andrea continued, Darren did his best to stay focused. She had no idea, of course, that his thoughts had shifted to the beautiful brunette who'd just entered the coffee shop. *Stop it, man. Be a gentleman.*

Thankfully, Candy and the other girls left after just a few minutes. Darren relaxed, finally able to be himself. Unfortunately, Andrea glanced at her watch and announced she had to leave.

"I've got a speaking engagement at seven, and I need to be a little early to set up my books."

"You're a writer. . .too?" He could hardly believe it. Was there anything the woman couldn't do?

"Yeah." She nodded and her cheeks turned pink. "Just a little book I wrote about allowing God back in the political arena. It's done pretty well on the New York Times bestseller list. I can't believe Brooke and Jason didn't mention it."

"I guess they wanted me to hear it from you. But, wow. A New York Times bestseller?"

"Aw, it's not a big deal." She rose to her feet and he joined her.

"No big deal?"

Andrea shrugged. "Trust me, in the circles I travel, having a book is nothing. The only thing that matters is making sure the right man—or woman—gets elected. And that's my real goal right now. Well, that and keeping my name before the public."

"Oh?"

"Might sound crazy. I'm not even all that interested in promoting myself or my book. But the more I can keep my name out there, the greater the chances I can help inner-city kids. That's my real passion."

"Right. Jason told me."

They headed toward the door of the coffee shop together. Andrea continued to share with enthusiasm in her voice. "I really am sorry that I have to leave. I was enjoying getting to know you."

"Same here."

Another glance at her watch caused her brow to wrinkle. "It's just that I'm speaking at a political fund-raiser tonight. Newark has plans for a wonderful new school of the arts for inner-city kids. They're planning to pattern it after a school in D.C. that I've worked with. Great things happening there. Wish I had the time to tell you all about it, but I've got to get going."

"Of course." He opened the door for her, and she extended her hand.

"Great to meet you, Darren." For a moment she looked directly into his eyes, and he thought he saw a glimmer of hope there.

"Great to meet you, too." He gave her hand a squeeze.

She disappeared in the direction of her rental car, and Darren stood in the open doorway, torn between returning inside for his half-filled cup of coffee and heading home to his empty house.

The coffee won out.

# *seven*

The next morning Darren dressed for work, his thoughts shifting back and forth from Andrea to Candy. Sure, last night's date was supposed to be about one woman, but how could he think straight, once Candy Carini walked in the room? He couldn't. And he'd wrestled with the sheets through the night, half-guilty about the fact that Candy had consumed his thoughts while he was on a date with Andrea, and half-wondering when he might see Candy again.

As he drove to work, Darren's cell phone rang. He pulled his car into a nearby parking lot to take the call. Darren recognized his friend Gary's voice at once. "Hey, Darren, you got a few minutes to talk?"

"Sure." He shifted the phone to the other ear.

"Just wanted to update you, in case you hadn't heard. Some of the guys are talking about picketing, claiming discrimination. What do you think of that idea?"

"Picketing? Discrimination?" He sighed. "I don't know, Gary."

His friend's voice tightened. "Easy for you to say. You're not the one being scrutinized. But I'll bet you'd be thinking about it a lot harder if you were walking a mile in my shoes right now."

"Ouch."

"Sorry." Gary released a sigh. "That was completely out of line, and I really am sorry. I guess it's just my disappointment speaking. I know my record with the company isn't as clean as yours. Frankly, I don't know anyone whose is. Still, this is tough, man."

Darren thought about Gary. . .his quick temper, the write-up he'd received for the way he'd snapped at his crew. One incident, in particular, had raised hairs. Gary had chewed out his first officer—a woman—a few weeks back. And, from what Darren had heard, the incident was unwarranted. Likely that had been enough to put his job at risk. This wasn't the first time, after all.

So, was Eastway really applying pressure because of rising fuel costs, or was that just what Gary wanted people to think? Regardless, picketing wasn't the answer, at least not until Darren knew all the details. Even then, what would the new pilots think if he linked arms with the other men? Likely, the new female pilots had no idea what they were walking into.

Thankfully, Gary got another call. Darren slapped his cell phone shut and decided to spend the remainder of his trip to the airport in prayer.

He arrived at the parking lot with plenty of time to spare. Determined not to let the phone conversation get the better of him, he boarded the plane. Craig, a flight attendant in his early thirties, caught his attention right away. "Morning, Cap'n. We've got a new first officer onboard today."

"Oh?" Darren shifted his flight bag to the other shoulder. "Who is he?"

"He's a *she*." Craig's eyebrows elevated. "And a mighty pretty she, if I do say so myself. She's a new hire, by the way. Looks a little nervous."

"She?" Darren released a slow breath. He knew in his gut just who "she" would be.

"Name's Candy Carini. Brooke says we're supposed to call her Cotton Candy just to get her riled up."

"On her first flight? I don't think so."

Craig's expression changed. "Hey, what's up with you? You're usually the jokester."

"I'm just saying there will be plenty of time for the funny stuff later. This is her first flight, and I'm sure her nerves are going to be an issue. She doesn't need any distractions."

"O—okay. No problem."

"So. . ." Darren looked around. "Where is she, anyway?"

"Inspecting the aircraft."

With his nerves slightly jumbled, Darren said his hellos to rest of the crew, then settled into his seat to prepare for departure.

❧

Though Candy had never flown for Eastway before today, she knew the drill. As copilot, she would carry out a visual inspection of the aircraft before entering the cockpit.

With some trepidation, she made her way around every square inch of the underbelly of the plane, checking for possible fuel leakage or hydraulic fluid dripping from pipelines. She scrutinized the landing gear and every tire, making sure they were in great condition, then inspected the engine turbine blades to make sure they were in tip-top shape. She continued on, going over everything with a fine-tooth comb. Thoroughly satisfied the aircraft was fit to fly, she made her way onboard.

Finally. The moment of truth. She approached the cockpit, surprised to find Darren Furst already seated. He turned to her with a brusque nod. She returned it, followed by a "Good morning, Captain."

"Morning."

*Okay, we're a man of few words this morning.* As she took her seat, Candy breathed a prayer for God's help. All of the years of preparation, and yet here she sat, scared out of her mind. Not that she needed to be. She'd simply been called on to copilot with Darren, and he certainly knew his stuff.

She watched as Darren marked items off a pretakeoff checklist. While waiting for approval from the ground control to push back from the gate and start the engines, Candy tried to make small talk. She made a funny comment about their common love of coffee, and he smiled. *Ah. A connection. Finally.*

At last the moment came to start the engines. Candy pushed aside all distractions and focused on the job at hand. Though she'd flown hundreds of times before, Candy felt her heart in her throat as Darren released the brake and applied power to accelerate down the runway. She knew how important this part was. The engines were at maximum power to lift the aircraft. The roar of the engines, coupled with Darren's voice as he spoke with the air traffic controllers, made things all the more exciting.

At just the right moment, Darren pulled back the yoke, lifting the nose of the plane. She leaned back against her seat, marveling at his calm assuredness. Seconds after takeoff, he retracted the landing gear. Candy looked for the three green landing-gear lights on the instrument panel to go off. *There. Done.*

The aircraft began to climb to its cruising altitude. This process took several minutes, but Candy didn't breathe a word. She knew the drill. Other than radio calls and checklists, they needed to keep a sterile cockpit. This was all too exciting to interrupt with conversation, anyway. *Thank You, Lord. I'm here! In the cockpit of an Eastway plane, copiloting. I'm living my dream. How can I ever thank You?* There were no words to describe how she felt in this moment.

When Darren took the intercom in hand to speak to the passengers over the PA, she listened to his spiel. "Good afternoon, ladies and gentlemen. This is your captain, Darren Furst." He stopped short of saying the rest, glancing her way with a shrug. A feeling of pure shame washed over her. Her words about his comedic one-liner must've intimidated him. Now he didn't feel free to be himself. Candy swallowed hard. *Sorry about that, Lord. I'll make it up to him, I promise.*

Once they'd reached their cruising altitude, Candy felt relaxed enough for a little small talk.

"Great work, Captain." She gave Darren a smile, hoping to bring the tension in the cockpit down a little.

"Thanks." He nodded in her direction. "I appreciate your help."

"That's what they pay me to do." *That's what they pay me to do. Wow.* She marveled at the fact that God had truly answered her prayers and given her the job of her dreams. Before, it had all seemed such a lofty goal. Flying. Like some elusive thing a child would say: One day, I'm going to fly up above the clouds!

"Cotton Candy, you've got your head in the clouds again," she whispered.

"Pardon?" Darren looked at her, his brow wrinkled. "Did you say something?"

"Oh, I just. . ." She looked at him with a smile. "Just something my dad used to say. He always thought I had my head in the clouds when I was a kid."

"Looks like you still do." He flashed a winning smile as he gestured to the clouds outside.

"Mm-hmm." Candy forced her attention to the instrument panel, where she busied herself. Still, she had a hard time containing the smile that tried to creep up.

The rest of the flight went smoothly. In fact, the time seemed to pass too fast. Candy did well with her part. And she soon entered into easy conversation with Darren. He was all business on takeoff, but once the plane was safely in the air, his comfort level seemed to improve.

Less than an hour later, they approached Chicago's busy O'Hare airport. To date, Candy had only seen this airport from a passenger's point of view. She'd certainly never analyzed the runways with a pilot's eye before.

The control tower directed their aircraft to land into the wind to bring down the ground speed. In spite of some crosswinds, Darren managed to land with skill and precision. He pulled back on the throttles, raised the spoilers to disrupt airflow over the wings, and reversed the thrust of the engines while applying the brakes. *Wow. Nice job.*

Darren picked up the intercom to speak to the passengers. He gave the usual thank-you-for-flying-with-us spiel, then turned to Candy and quirked a brow before adding, "We'd like to ask that you remain seated until we reach the gate, ladies and gentlemen. To my knowledge, no Eastway passenger ever beat the plane to the gate."

She couldn't help but laugh. *Thank goodness. He's himself again.*

Within minutes they'd taxied into their parking bay. After shutting things down, Darren turned to her. "Let's go say good-bye to our passengers." He rose, then extended his hand to help her stand. Something about the feel of his hand in hers sent a feeling of warmth rushing through her. This was a man she could trust. . .not just with her emotions, but her very life.

She tagged along behind him as they joined Brooke and the rest of the crew to wave good-bye to their passengers.

"Great flight, Cap'n," Craig said, when the last of the passengers left.

"And great flight to you, too." Brooke gave Candy an admiring look. "How did it feel, being in the cockpit?"

"Wonderful." Should she add that being there with Darren gave her the security she needed to make it through her first Eastway flight?

"Now we get to turn around and do it all over again." Brooke glanced at her watch. "We'll depart for Newark in less than an hour. Should arrive just before six. Anyone up to dinner at DiMarco's after? Best Italian food in Newark."

"Italian food?" Candy shrugged. "My personal favorite."

Darren looked her way with a smile. "If you're in, I'm in."

*Oh yeah, I'm in all right.*

"Well then, when we get to Newark, we'll fly this coop." His eyes sparkled with excitement. . .an invitation, perhaps?

"Mm-hmm." With this man at the helm, she might just be willing to fly to the moon.

# eight

At six forty-five that same evening, Candy found herself seated around a table at DiMarco's Italian restaurant with several fellow employees—Brooke, Shawneda, Darren, and a friend of Shawneda's named Teresa. The delicious smell of garlic hung in the air, and everywhere she looked, people dined on pizza, pasta, and other goodies.

Glancing at her new friends, she had to admit, there was a certain camaraderie here, one she loved already. These people were truly becoming family. . .and in such a short time. And now, as they sat with menus in hand, Candy marveled at the fact that she'd only known them weeks and not years.

"I'm so glad you like Italian food," Brooke said, leaning her way. "I can't live without it. It's in the Antonelli blood."

"Oh, I love it." Candy nodded, eyeing a plate of pasta as the waiter carried it by. "I'm a Carini, after all. Grew up in a fairly traditional Italian family."

"Really?" Darren looked her way. "So, what are you going to order? I think I'm going to have the spaghetti and meatballs."

"Just like a guy." Shawneda rolled her eyes. "You could eat spaghetti any night of the week, and you order it in a restaurant? C'mon. Live dangerously. Climb out of the box. Order something different for a change."

"Different?" He looked at her, perplexed. "But. . .I like spaghetti."

"Yeah, me, too." Candy shrugged. "But I'll bet the meatballs aren't as good as my mom's."

Darren gave her an inquisitive look. "So, your mom is a good cook?"

"Oh, the best." Candy smiled as she thought about the

many ways her mother excelled above most other moms she knew. "You name it, she can make it. Main course, desserts, and you should see her ice cream cakes. She sells a lot of those at the store."

"Wow, she sounds great."

"Oh, she is. I truly think she's one of the biggest blessings in my life. And she's one of those women who's great at everything. Pop says she's got the Midas touch. But then again, he's always been the first one to sing her praises. I love it."

"Ah."

His expression shifted from interest to something. . .almost sad. Candy couldn't put her finger on it. Had she said something wrong? "So, tell me about your mom. Is she a good cook?"

"I guess so, but she never really enjoyed cooking, and I guess it showed in the food. It was good, don't get me wrong. Just not. . ." He paused and shook his head. Clearly, he did not want to be talking about this. "Anyway, our dinner table experiences weren't the best in town. But it didn't have a lot to do with the food."

Candy quickly changed the direction of the conversation. "Well, I'm not great in the kitchen, either. I don't mind admitting it. I've tried my hand at cooking, but I've burned half the stuff I attempted. Maybe I'll get better in time."

"You just need the right man to cook for." Brooke winked.

Candy did her best not to roll her eyes. *Please. Finding the right guy isn't going to make me want to cook.*

Then again, how did she know? Maybe finding the right guy would make her want to do all of the things she hadn't enjoyed before.

Like now, for instance. She'd never been great at opening up and sharing in a group. As the middle child, sitting quietly while others talked around her had pretty much been the norm. But today, with Darren at her side, she was chattering about dozens of things. Maybe it was just the postflight nerves, but something gave her the added zeal to throw her two cents' worth in at nearly every turn.

"I'm glad to see this side of you," Brooke said, when Candy paused for breath. "I was starting to wonder if you'd ever come out of your shell."

Candy giggled. "I guess it took getting that first flight out of my system. But I think you're going to see a whole different side of me now."

Looking at Darren, she had to wonder if he would like the new and improved Candy Carini. Not that what he thought really mattered. Right? After all, he was just a fellow employee, nothing more.

Looking into his eyes she realized for the first time that she actually wanted it to be more.

☙

As they waited on their food, the conversation shifted to the flight. Darren waited for just the right moment to share his thoughts with Candy. When the other girls entered into an exaggerated and somewhat annoying discussion about handbags, he turned to her and spoke quietly. "I just wanted to tell you that you did a great job today. I was impressed. And you looked at ease."

Candy's eyes sparkled as she responded. "Thanks. Don't know if I mentioned it to you or not, but I got in some of my flight hours working for a cargo carrier. I was with them a little over a year."

"Really?" He gave her an admiring look. "I got my hours in as a charter pilot in California."

"Same with a lot of my friends. But cargo jobs were easier to come by in Arizona." She shrugged. "Probably not as exciting, though."

"But it kept you in the air." He gave her a smile.

"Right. And anything that keeps you in the air is a good thing."

"Amen to that." He paused a moment. "You're a Christian, right?"

"Yes." She nodded, but quirked a brow, likely wondering where he was headed with this line of questioning.

"I haven't met a lot of other Christian pilots. A few, but not many. Just wondering. . ."

"What?" She gave him a curious look.

"Well, when I'm flying, I feel. . .closer to God. Does that make sense?"

The edges of her lips turned up as she responded. "Makes a lot of sense. It's one of the things I love most about flying. There's something about being up there in the clouds that makes Him seem so close. Like I could reach out and touch Him."

*I couldn't have put it better myself.* "There's a scripture I love. I think it's in Isaiah. It's the one about mounting up with eagle's wings."

"Sure. Of course." She gave him an inquisitive look.

"I waited a long time for the opportunity to fly," he said. "Dreamed about it when I was a kid. I was always the one jumping off the roof, pretending I could fly."

"Me, too." The dazzling smile that followed her words nearly caused him to forget the rest of his story.

*Sounds like we have a lot in common.* "Well, when I'm in the cockpit, I feel like everything I waited for was for a purpose. Like I'm that eagle, taking flight. Like nothing can stop me."

"Wow." Candy gave him a look of admiration, then paused for a moment, a thoughtful look on her face. "Whenever I'm flying, I think of that verse in Psalms about God mounting the cherubim and flying." She quoted the rest from memory: " 'He soared on the wings of the wind.' " Her eyes filled with tears. "Might sound crazy, but it's overwhelming to think that God is right there, flying alongside me. I sense His presence most when I'm in the air."

"Man. Me, too." Darren forgot just about everything he'd planned to say next. Looking into Candy's tear-filled eyes, he found himself completely overwhelmed—not just with her passion for flying, but her passion for the Lord.

Off to the side, something distracted him. Brooke looked back and forth between them, her eyes narrowed. Darren finally turned to her to ask, "What?"

"You two." She shook her head.

"What about us?" Candy took a sip from her glass of water.

"You're a match made in heaven. And this time, I mean that quite literally."

Thankfully, Darren didn't have time to comment. The waitress chose that moment to appear with their food. He caught Candy's eye as the steaming bowls of spaghetti and meatballs were placed before him. She gave him a little wink and his heart seemed to turn itself inside out.

After Darren prayed over the food, he turned his attention to Candy once again. "So, you were a cargo pilot."

"Yes. Got in a lot of hours. A little on the boring side, though. Hurry up and wait stuff. I also did a short stint as a skydiving pilot."

"Really. Ever witness any accidents?" He took a bite of the spaghetti, waiting for her response.

She shook her head. "No, but a couple of close calls. We had a guy who had to use his backup chute. And the worst was a woman who got tangled up in a tree. She was pretty scraped up, but no broken bones, thankfully."

Darren was just about to ask her if she'd ever jumped, but Brooke interrupted him. "I think you'd have to be nuts to jump out of a plane. I can't imagine doing it. . .on purpose, anyway."

"Well, how else would you do it?" Candy asked. Everyone laughed, including Darren. *See there. She's got a great sense of humor, too.*

Brooke put her hand up. "I'm just saying, in our line of work, it's better to keep all arms and legs inside the plane, not out."

"Yeah," Darren said, "but there's something about the idea

of free-falling that's pretty amazing. Letting go of everything. Releasing every care, every anxiety. . ."

"Releasing anxiety?" Candy looked at him, her eyes wide. "Jumping out of a plane will help me release my anxieties?"

Okay. So there was his answer as to whether or not she'd ever jumped. Obviously not. "Well, you need to try it sometime. I think it's a blast. Very freeing."

"Darren's always coming up with kooky ideas." Brooke laughed. "But usually they're not life-threatening. One time he came up with this off-the-wall plan for our crew out of Chicago. He bought those goofy-looking fake teeth for all of the flight attendants. You know the ones I'm talking about? They look awful."

"Yes, I think so." Candy shrugged.

Darren groaned, realizing just how nutty this story would make him look.

Brooke continued, more animated than before. "Well, at the end of the flight, all the flight attendants turned toward the front of the plane to put the teeth in, then turned back to the passengers. When we opened our mouths. . ." Brooke started laughing so hard, she could barely continue. "When we opened our mouths, Darren came over the PA and told the passengers that Eastway had a crummy dental program. Told them to keep flying with us so the company could afford to get better coverage."

Candy chuckled as she looked at Darren. "That's hysterical."

At her words, his concerns vanished. *She thinks I'm funny.* That changed everything.

"And then he did this really horrible thing to his fabulous crew members once," Brooke continued. "This one really took the cake. We were on an evening flight, and the lights in the cabin were down. So, Darren comes on the PA and tells the passengers he's turned down the lights to enhance the appearance of the flight attendants."

"Ouch." Candy giggled.

"Hey, I thought it was funny," Darren said with a shrug. "And the passengers did, too. But. . .I ended up apologizing later. Should've stopped myself before poking fun at my own crew."

"Nah." Brooke laughed and dismissed it with the wave of a hand. "We all thought it was a hoot. In fact, we think all of Darren's jokes are funny, even the goofy ones. In fact, they're the funniest of all."

Darren took a bite of his spaghetti, finally starting to relax. Maybe Candy wouldn't think less of him, after all.

"So, let me ask you a question." She turned to face him. "Were you always the funny guy? Like, class clown? Where did all this humor come from, anyway?"

The conversation seemed to shift a bit as his gaze tipped downward. When he finally looked up, Darren said, "My parents didn't always get along. My mom. . .well, let's just say she wasn't easy to live with. And my dad pretty much checked out when she turned on him, which was a lot. So I tried to infuse humor whenever things got tense. And, um. . . they got tense pretty often."

"So you were the buffer?"

"I guess I've always believed God can use humor to lift people's spirits. I never know who's going to end up on one of my flights. But I pray before every one. And you never know. Someone might be having a terrible day, but then I give them something to laugh at and they feel better."

"And he does make them feel better." Brooke gave an emphatic nod, then turned Darren's way. "It's amazing how many passengers tell me how great they think you are."

He offered a quiet, "Thanks."

"And I hear Fred thinks you're pretty cool, too."

Darren groaned.

"Fred?" Candy gave him a funny look. "Who's Fred?"

"My new goldfish. Jason decided I was lonely, so he bought me a fish. Just brought it over a few days ago. Kind of a lonely little guy, swimming in that great big tank."

"Well, I'm just glad to finally hear there's a fish in the tank," Brooke said. "Never could figure out why you had an empty fish tank in your living room."

*Same reason I have an empty house. I've got no one to put in it.*

Darren cleared his throat. "Well, it's not empty anymore. Fred keeps me company now."

"I'd like to meet him someday." Candy gave him an unpretentious smile.

*We will see to that.* Darren took a bite of his pasta and tried to swallow down the remainder of his embarrassment with it.

The conversation quieted for a couple of minutes as everyone ate. Brooke finally broke the silence with an announcement.

"Before I forget. . .remember I promised to set up a trip to Atlantic City for the singles ministry?"

Candy looked across the table at her with a surprised look on her face. "You're going to my old stomping ground on a field trip? I don't remember hearing about it."

"Well, I'm doing it for Darren, really. He's never been to the boardwalk."

"Oh, wow." Candy looked at him with a stunned expression. "Well, you've missed out on a lot, then. The arcades, the shops, the hotels, the water. It's a pretty amazing place."

He shrugged. "I'm from the West Coast. I guess I've just had a hard time adjusting to the Atlantic. The Pacific is. . ." He sighed. "Well, where I lived in Southern California, it was pretty unbelievable."

"Trust me, we've got some pretty beaches on the East Coast, too," Candy said. As she began to describe the colors of the water against the white sand, Darren found himself hanging on every word. It had nothing to do with the description of the beaches. No, he could care less about beaches right now. All that mattered in this moment was the look of pure joy on the face of the prettiest pilot he'd ever met.

# nine

Candy spent the rest of the meal laughing and talking with the others. The time passed far too quickly. By the time they finished their meal and the conversation, it was nine thirty.

Darren excused himself from the group. "I've got a long day ahead of me tomorrow."

"Me, too," Candy said. As the other girls murmured their agreement and began to get up from the table, Candy started to push her chair back, but he rose and helped her. *Wow. Okay, then. Either he's just incredibly friendly or he's paying me special attention.*

They said their good-byes and parted ways, but Candy couldn't stop thinking about Darren. All the way back to the apartment, her mind reeled. She replayed the whole day—the part on the plane and especially the part at dinner, where he gazed at her with such tenderness in his eyes.

After Brooke, Shawneda, and Candy arrived at their apartment, Candy slipped into her PJs, then knocked on Brooke's bedroom door.

"Come in."

She went inside, grateful that Shawneda was in the shower. Candy wanted to talk to Brooke alone, away from the crowd for a change. Brooke gestured for her to sit on the bed, so she did.

"So, tell me more about Darren." Candy hesitated. "He seems a little. . ."

"Soft?"

Candy nodded. "And funny." She paused, thinking through her words before speaking them. "It's so strange. When we're at church or in a restaurant or something, he's completely relaxed. But around some of the guys on the plane—like

Craig, for instance—I noticed he was a little more guarded. The first few minutes of our flight today he was pretty cool toward me. He softened up, but it took a few minutes."

"Ah, well. . ." Brooke hesitated. "There's a reason for that."

"Really?"

Brooke sighed, and her gaze shifted for a moment. As she looked back in Candy's direction, she said, "I think it's a little complicated, actually."

"Tell me."

"Well, Darren talked to Jason about all of this just a few days ago. He's upset because a couple of pilots have lost their jobs at Eastway recently and others were hired on to take their place."

"Oh." Candy's heart felt like it hit her toes. "I had no idea they were letting people go. Do you know why?"

Brooke drew in a deep breath. "Jason said it has something to do with rising fuel costs, but I'm not so sure."

"Then why hire new pilots?" None of this made any sense.

"Well, they're hiring women, which has the guys worked up. They're speculating it has something to do with a quota, which is ridiculous. Eastway doesn't work like that. Their hiring practices have never come under question like this." Brooke's gaze shifted to the window, then back again. "But, look, don't take it personally. This is just scuttlebutt. The rumor mill at work. We don't know any of this for sure."

"Wow. So what should I do?"

"Just be yourself. And fly straight. Do your best." Brooke hesitated a moment. "But, Candy, be prepared for something, okay?"

"What?"

"Craig told me some of the men were thinking of making a bigger deal out of the incoming female pilots than they should. Involving the union. Picketing, even. They're all worked up and followed after Gary. He's the pied piper here, and a suspicious one, at best. He's had his share of problems with Eastway, but never admits when he's done something wrong."

Candy's heart suddenly felt like lead. "D–do you think Darren would join them?"

"I can't imagine it, but you never know. He's done his best to befriend Gary, mostly to witness to him. And like I said, Gary's the one who's the most worked up." Brooke sighed. "If you ask me, he had it coming. I've flown with him in the past and seen his true colors. He's pretty short with the crew and even with the tower. He was written up before, and his attitude doesn't seem to be improving."

"Ah." Candy relaxed a little bit at this news.

"Right. You get it. And I'm sure you've heard that runway incidents are up at Newark Liberty. Statistics aren't good. So, everyone's on guard. But Gary's got the guys in a frenzy, so be prepared. There's nothing worse than a band of angry men."

A shiver ran down Candy's spine. She'd run into her share of frustrated male pilots over the years, for sure. In flight school, and even on the job in Arizona. Still, she'd never seen them protest in a public way, like the kind of thing Brooke was talking about. Looked like she had plenty to pray about.

"Hey, you two look way too serious." Shawneda came out of the bathroom in some crazy-looking Pink Panther pajamas and her hair in a towel. "We need to lighten things up a little." She pulled the towel from her hair and began smacking them with it.

After a few minutes of laughter, Brooke spoke up. "Shawneda, I think you should've been born a boy."

"Hey now. Watch what you're saying. I'm a girlie girl." She smacked Brooke with the towel once again.

Still laughing, Candy excused herself and headed to her bedroom. Thankfully, Lilly was working a late-night shift, so she had the room to herself. As she climbed into bed, Candy pondered Brooke's words. *So, Darren is secretly upset with me for potentially taking a job away from one of the guys.*

That changed everything. Absolutely everything.

❧

Darren had just settled into bed when the phone rang. Looking at the caller ID, he noticed Jason's number.

He answered with the words, "You're up late."

"Yeah, I hear I missed a great time at dinner. Brooke filled me in. Wish I could've come."

"It was nice."

"So, how's Fred?" Jason's voice had a humorous edge to it.

"Lonely. But I think he's adjusting."

"Mm-hmm. Maybe you need to buy him a girlfriend. That way he's not alone in that tank of his. Oh, and speaking of females. . .Brooke told me that Candy copiloted today. How did that go?"

Darren leaned back against the pillows, noticing for the first time how bare his bedroom walls looked. *I really should hang a few pictures in here.* Snapping back to attention, he said, "Really well, actually. She knows her stuff. It's rare to find an incoming pilot this secure."

"Especially a woman?"

Darren groaned. "Look, I don't have a problem with female pilots. Just because Gary and the others are getting all worked up doesn't mean I have to."

"Ah. So getting to know her has changed your thinking, then."

"What do you mean?"

"I mean you were a little more adamant before. Tonight it seems like you're softening."

"According to your fiancée, I'm nothing but a marshmallow anyway."

"No, you've got a backbone. It's apparent to me. And there's nothing wrong with being nice. A lot of people I know are nice."

"Jason, *you're* the nice one." Darren laughed. "I guess I just didn't expect these incoming female pilots to be so. . .good at what they do. I was thinking they'd be a little sloppier. Some of the incoming pilots are, especially the nervous ones."

"But not Candy?"

"Nope. Not so far. And I guess I expected her to be really aggressive. More demanding. And Candy's nothing like that. She's. . ."

"Yeah, Brooke told me she's pretty great. So, are you thinking about—"

"No. You know my policy. No way."

"So, let me ask you a question. You're only interested in soft-spoken women? Don't want someone with chutzpa?"

"What are you talking about?"

"Well, give me a woman with spunk any day."

"Um, you've *got* a woman with spunk."

"Yeah, I do. No doubt about that." Jason laughed.

"And Candy has plenty of spunk, too," Darren added. "I also saw her business side in the cockpit today. She's really a well-balanced woman."

"Well, there you go. A well-balanced woman." Jason laughed. "Why does that surprise you so much?"

Darren sighed. "Look, Jason, we've known each other awhile, but you don't really know a lot about my background. It's kind of skewed my view of women."

"Then fill me in."

Darren paused a moment before explaining. "Look, here's the thing. My dad—I love him—but my mom's got him wrapped around her finger, and I don't mean that in a good way. She calls all the shots in that household. Always has." His mind reeled backward in time. He could see his father now in his mail carrier's uniform, walking in the door after a long day on his feet. Could hear his mother's voice, drilling him about this or that. She never asked him anything. Always told him. And never in a nice voice.

Jason's voice interrupted Darren's thoughts. "So you're looking for just the opposite? Is that why you're so relieved Candy's a softie like you?"

Darren sighed. He'd never come out and said it, but yes.

Not that he wanted to tell anyone what to do, but it would be nice to have a woman's respect. And not because of anything he happened to do for a living. It wasn't about that.

"I'm just saying aggressive isn't terribly appealing to me, particularly from a woman." *And if you knew how aggressive my mother was—is—you'd understand.*

"Doesn't sound like that's what you're saying to me. I think you're really wishing your dad had been more aggressive."

*Ouch.*

"So, have you forgiven him?"

"Forgiven my dad?" Darren's jaw tightened as he contemplated Jason's words. "Why would I need to forgive my dad? He's a great guy. My mom is the one who—"

"Darren, listen. I don't know your parents and don't want to presume anything about them. But in a relationship that's completely out of balance—where one person clearly holds the reins—the guilt is on both sides. Men need to stand up and be men. Take responsibility. But that doesn't mean women have to roll over and play dead when a man walks into the room."

"Well, I never said—"

"No, but you're thinking it. You're okay as long as no one rocks the boat. And maybe you thought Candy and these other incoming female pilots might do just that. But, so what if they had? Maybe the boat needs to be rocked."

Darren sighed. "Maybe. Never thought about that."

"Well, think about it. And Darren, it's not just your view on women that's skewed. You've spent too much time analyzing both sexes. I think you're secretly worried that you're not aggressive enough to handle a strong woman, but you are."

*I hope so.*

"So, your dad was too soft. And maybe you're worried you're a little soft, too. But I know you. I've watched you for years. Your strength is in God, not yourself. And that's a good thing. I think you're more balanced than you know. Soft on the outside, tough on the inside."

"Never thought about it that way."

"Just don't go too far out of your way to become something other than what you are, especially if these guys at Eastway get all riled up. You don't have to prove anything to anyone."

"Right."

"And don't worry about the female thing." Jason laughed. "God's going to bring you just the right person to balance you out. She won't be aggressive like your mother. You'll see to that. But she won't be a piece of fluff, either. She'll have a backbone. And you'll love that about her. So, get ready."

*Oh, I'm ready all right.* As he ended the call, Darren realized about just how ready he was.

# ten

The following Saturday morning, Darren paced his house, a nervous wreck. "Just call her, man. It's not rocket science. She's just a woman."

He punched in Candy's number and, thankfully, she answered on the third ring.

"Candy? This is Darren," he managed. *Why are my palms sweating?*

"Darren, hi. Something happen I need to know about?" At once he picked up on a hint of anxiety in her voice.

"No, nothing happening at work, if that's what you mean. I, um. . .well, I have a friend who has a Cessna 400, and he's wondering if I want to take it out for a spin. I thought maybe you might like to come with me."

"Come fly with you?"

"Yes." There. He'd said it. Now, if she would just come back with an affirmative answer. . .

"Sounds like fun. Where? When?"

*Whew.* "This afternoon. Do you know where Essex County airport is?"

"Sort of. I know it's not far. Maybe northwest of here?"

"Yes. Won't take us long to get there, and I'll do the driving. I'll pick you up in an hour. . .unless that's too soon."

"An hour?" She paused and he almost cratered while waiting for her response. She finally came back with, "Um, sure. I've been out running errands this morning and look. . .well, not great."

As if that were possible. "Just come as you are," he said.

They ended the call and Darren flew into action. If things went as planned, Candy Carini would see a whole new side to him today. . .hopefully one she couldn't resist. He picked out a nice shirt to wear. Blue. Someone once told him it brought out the color of his eyes. He'd never forgotten that. And he spent a little extra time working on his hair today. No point in scaring her with unruly waves. He leaned in close to the mirror to examine every square inch of his face. *Ah. Missed a spot shaving. Better remedy that.*

As he prepared to leave the house, Darren stopped off at the fish tank to look at Fred. "Hey, little guy." The forlorn goldfish swam around the tank in solitude making *Ooo, Ooo, Ooo* faces. "I feel your pain. Should I get you a fish friend? Maybe a female? Someone in a great shade of orange?"

After no response from Fred, Darren hit the road. There would be plenty of time to worry about the fish's love life later. Right now he'd better focus on his own.

ॐ

Candy touched up her makeup and double-checked her outfit in the mirror before Darren arrived. She could hardly wait to spend time with him one-on-one, away from the crowd. She marveled over how much her feelings for him seemed to be changing. Thinking of how she'd judged him that first day on the plane now brought nothing but shame. Any lingering questions she'd had about his flying abilities had been answered in the cockpit. And certainly, from their many times together in a group environment, his love for God had come shining through. Of course, there was that thing about the male pilots losing their jobs. . .

*No, I'm not going to go there.*

She pushed aside any troubling thoughts and prepared for her date with Darren. How wonderful it would be, to hit the skies in a small plane once again. Surely—after hearing her story the other night—he'd planned this day just for her. And she couldn't wait.

The doorbell rang promptly at 1:30 p.m., just as he'd said. Candy answered with a smile on her face. "You're right on time."

"Yes, I. . ." He looked at her, his eyes widening. "Wow."

His one word caused heat to rise to her cheeks. "Thanks. I wasn't sure what to wear."

"Anything but the uniform would be just fine." He laughed. "If you're like I am, you change the minute you get home. It's pretty confining."

She shrugged. "Oh, I don't know. I kind of like it. But I'm pretty new and all."

"Right. Well, that blouse is. . .wow. And I've never seen you in jeans before. They suit you."

"Thank you." His charming and somewhat embarrassing words made her feel like a high schooler all over again. And he didn't look half bad in that blue shirt, either. Really made his eyes pop. But, should she tell him? Did women say things like that to guys? Not on a first date, likely.

Thankfully, she never had time to carry through with the idea. He led the way out of the apartment and toward the parking lot. When they reached the car, he opened the front passenger door for her.

"Thank you, kind sir." She gave him a wink. *Where did that come from?*

"You're more than welcome." He returned the wink and closed the door.

Butterflies rose up in Candy's stomach, and they fluttered in greater anticipation as she glanced in the backseat and saw a large wicker picnic basket. *If he's got our lunch in there, I'm going to marry him today, whether he asks or not.*

Minutes later Darren pulled the car out onto the expressway, headed northwest.

"I haven't been to Essex County airport in ages," he said. "But my friend Jimmy works out there, and he's pretty proud of this new bird of his. It's a Cessna 400."

"I'll bet. I wouldn't mind owning a Cessna myself. But I like the Cessna 208. You can seat nine."

"Really?" Darren gave her a funny look. "That's funny.

I was about to say the same thing."

"Well, I have a big family. My parents, two sisters, a brother-in-law, and a baby on the way."

"A baby on the way?"

"My sister. Taffie."

"Oh, right. The older sister."

"Yep. I've always thought it would be a blast to be able to fly my whole family away on a vacation someplace." She sighed as she contemplated the improbabilities of getting everyone in the family together at the same time in the same place. "Who knows. Maybe it'll happen someday."

"I hope so. Sounds like fun. I mean. . .if you're okay with me taking one of the leftover seats."

"Well, of course. We wouldn't dream of going without you." *Now, where did that come from?*

They lit into a conversation about small planes, chatting easily as he drove. Several times she caught him looking at her out of the corner of his eye. Unlike that day in the cockpit, he seemed more relaxed. More himself.

Candy wanted to ask about the situation with the men at Eastway, but decided this wouldn't be the time or the place. If he wanted to talk about all of that, surely he would bring it up. But why ruin a perfectly wonderful afternoon?

They arrived at Essex County at two fifteen. As soon as Darren pulled his car into the parking lot, Candy's excitement grew.

"You ready for this?" he asked, as he turned to her with a boyish grin.

"I can't wait."

"So, you want to fly. . .or jump?"

"J–jump?" Her heart began to race. Jumping certainly wasn't in her plans.

"Hey, you told me you flew a skydiving plane. Right? I thought maybe you might like to—"

"Oh no!" She put her hands up, terrified at the idea. "It's

one thing to fly the plane, another to jump out of it."

He chuckled as he got out of the car and came around to her side. Opening the door, he said, "Well, if you change your mind, let me know. I have it on good authority Jimmy will take over the flying if we decide to skydive. And I'm a consummate skydiver. Love it, in fact."

Candy shook off the idea right away. She'd never confessed this to a soul. . .didn't know if she ever would. . .but the idea of skydiving terrified her. Too many variables. No, she'd stick to piloting, thank you very much.

For the next half hour, Candy and Darren made the rounds from hangar to hangar to look at the various planes.

"Hey, check out this. . . ." She pointed to a single engine SkyCatcher. "What do you think of that?"

"Small." He shook his head. "After flying for Eastway, these planes look microscopic to me."

"Same here. But it's funny. That first flight with Eastway, the plane felt huge. Now it's just right."

"You sound like Goldilocks."

"What?"

"You know. This chair is too big. This one's too small. This one is just right." He started laughing and before long she joined in.

"I guess it's all a matter of perspective."

"Yep." He paused at a small jet. "Now we're talking. This is what I'd buy, if I could." He gave it a closer look. "I'd run a charter service back and forth from New York to DC. Can you imagine my clientele during an election year?"

"It would be crazy, but fun." She climbed inside the small aircraft and looked around. "This reminds me of being in Arizona. I flew a jet about this size once." She settled into the pilot's seat, feeling right at home. "Oh yeah." A couple of minutes later she emerged with a smile on her face. "So, where's this 400 we're supposed to fly?"

"Funny you should ask," a male voice rang out from behind

them. "I'd just had to put her out of service. Engine trouble."

She turned to see a man, slightly older than Darren, approaching. Must be Jimmy.

"Oh no." Darren groaned. "So we drove out here for nothing."

"Oh, not for nothing." Candy drew near and gave him her best it-was-worth-it-anyway look. "It's been great, just seeing all of these planes and being at a small airport again. Reminds me of where I've come from. And I don't mind about the 400. Really."

Darren made introductions, but Candy could read the disappointment in his eyes.

"I can still take you up in the SkyCatcher," Jimmy said. "She's a beauty."

"No, don't worry about it. We can still look around, and I brought lunch. . . . "

Candy gave him a reassuring look. "I think that sounds great. Really. We can fly anytime."

"Well, tell me if you change your mind," Jimmy said. "In the meantime, if you're interested in climbing aboard the Chariot for a view of the cockpit, feel free."

"The Chariot?" Candy's confusion grew.

"Oh, that's what I call my 400. She's my Chariot. Only, not today. She's just outside the hangar, drinking up some sunshine." He led them around the side of the building.

Candy gasped as she saw the beautiful plane with THE CHARIOT emblazoned in gold letters on the side. "Oh, she's gorgeous. Look at those colors."

"And great lettering. Jimmy did all of the detailing himself."

"Flattery will get you everywhere." Jimmy winked. "You kids go on and climb aboard. I've got to get back up to the office. Stop by after you've had your lunch and we'll chat awhile."

"Thanks, Jimmy." Darren reached to shake his hand.

"No problem." Jimmy headed off toward the terminal, and Darren gazed at Candy with renewed hope in his eyes.

"Want to climb aboard?"

"Do I ever!"

"Well, madame. . .your chariot awaits." After a quick glance at the words on the side of the plane, he added, "Literally."

# eleven

Darren's frustrations over the grounded plane lifted the minute he saw the joy in Candy's expression. Clearly she didn't mind if they only saw the view from the ground. She was content to do just that.

He helped her onboard, then joined her. Once inside, they sat together in silence for a moment, looking things over. Candy finally spoke up. "If I closed my eyes, I could see myself back in Arizona. What about you?"

"Hmm. Well, I guess I could see myself back in California. I haven't flown many small planes since then."

"Okay, let's do it." She gave him a playful smile.

"Do what?"

"Close our eyes and pretend."

"Um. . .okay." He shrugged, then squeezed his eyes shut.

"What do you see?" she asked after a minute.

"The inside of my eyelids?"

Candy laughed. "No, where do you see yourself flying? Use your imagination. If you could fly anywhere in the world. . .if money and time were no object, where would you go?"

"Oh, that's easy." He relaxed a bit, his eyes still shut. "I've always wanted to fly over the countryside in England. In a plane just like this one."

"We're there right now." The enthusiasm in Candy's voice prompted him to play along. "Just use your imagination. What do you see?"

"Hmm." He paused a moment to think about it, never opening his eyes. "I see the tops of country houses with smoke coming from the chimneys."

"Sounds amazing. What else?"

Darren opened one eye long enough to sneak a peek of her beautiful face. Sure enough, her eyes were still closed. She was taking this game very seriously. "Well, I see green. Everywhere. Green rolling hills. And a river. It's beautiful. Oh, and look. . .there's a castle. With a moat."

"It's a shame I left my ball gown and tiara at home." She sighed. "We'll have to miss the fun. But what else do you see?"

"Well. . ." He stretched his imagination. "I think we're coming into a city. Oh, it's London. Look there. It's Big Ben. Want a closer look?"

"Sure!"

He let out a whooshing sound. "Whew. Barely missed it. But it's seven forty-five London time, in case you missed that."

"No, I saw it." She laughed. "You're really good at this."

*I wouldn't be caught dead doing it in front of any of the guys I know, but thanks.*

Deciding to play along, Darren turned the question on her. "So, your turn. Where do you want to go?"

"Hmm. Well, I've always wanted to fly way out over the ocean," she said. "We didn't see a lot of water in Arizona."

"So, where are you taking me?" He smiled as soon as the words were spoken. Darren knew where Candy Carini was taking him, of course. Right over the edge. Into the vast unknown. Into uncharted territory, places his heart had never visited. Not that he minded. He'd play along, if it meant being with her. And besides, he was rather enjoying this.

"I think I'll fly us over the Hawaiian Islands," she said, her voice taking on a dreamy sound. "We'll start with the big island, okay?"

"Sure."

"Oh, do you see that?"

"See what?" He opened one eye again, half expecting to really see something.

"That volcano. It's erupting off in the distance. Made the plane shake. Oh, man. I've got to get us out of here. Look at that ash." Her tone grew more soothing. "But don't worry about that now. We're back out over the water. It's gorgeous. Have you ever in your life seen water like that before? I've never seen that color. Would you call that teal or cerulean?"

"Cerulean?" His eyes opened instinctively. "What in the world is cerulean?"

"A shade of blue. How can anyone *not* believe in God when they see a color like that? Close your eyes, now. No peeking."

Her eyes were closed tight. *How in the world could she. . . ?*

"Oh, hold on!" she called out. "We're about to fly over a really nice hotel with a beautiful white sand beach. I want to see if I recognize any movie stars. Oh, look right there. I'm pretty sure that's. . .aw, never mind. It's not her. Tell the paparazzi to put their cameras away. They're always such a nuisance, don't you think? Popping up behind trees and bushes just to snag a photograph."

Darren opened his eyes and sat straight up in his seat. "Candy, can I ask you a question?"

Her eyes popped open and she looked at him, seemingly confused. "What?"

"Did you play games like this when you were a kid?"

She gave him a sheepish look. "M—maybe."

"Mm-hmm." He paused a moment. "So, all that stuff about you having your head in the clouds came from games like this."

"I suppose." She shrugged. "How come?"

"Oh, I don't know." An uneasy feeling came over him as a new revelation surfaced. "You're a daydreamer, but in a really nice sort of way. Me. . ." He paused, wondering if she would be bothered by his next words. "When I was a kid, there wasn't a lot of time for daydreams. My mom was a taskmaster. Always after me to get things done. I hardly remember any free time. Certainly no time to allow my mind to wander like this."

"Ah." She gave him a sympathetic look. "My parents were. . . *are* both hard workers. But they certainly gave us kids room to dream. My mom always said I was like Joseph from the Old Testament. . .dreaming the day away. Talking about things that seemed improbable. Oh, but you should meet my dad. He's the biggest dreamer of them all."

"I wish I could say the same." Darren exhaled. . .a little too loud. "But anyway, I stopped dreaming a long time ago. Maybe that's what wrong with me."

"What's wrong with you?" She gave him a curious look. "Who says there's anything wrong with you?"

He pondered that a moment. Yeah. Who said there was anything wrong with him?

Candy gave him a look so sweet he felt the grip around his heart give way at once. "Darren, you can't let whatever happened to you as a child keep you from being all God wants you to be. And it's not too late to dream. There's still plenty of time. . .for both of us."

*Yes, there is.* Staring into her eyes, he truly believed it.

"C'mon, there's one more place I want to take you. Close your eyes."

Darren suppressed a laugh as he jumped into the game once again.

"I've always wanted to see Tuscany." Candy sighed. "Oh, but Darren, look. It's so much prettier than I thought it would be. Do you see those colors? This is the most amazing landscape I've ever seen. Would you like to go to Rome next, or Venice?"

"Venice. I've always wanted to see the canals."

"Me, too. My grandfather was from Italy, you know."

"Really?" He opened his eyes and stared at her, surprised. "I didn't realize that."

"Yes. He came to America in the '30s, just before the Second World War. His family was originally from a small village in central Italy. So when I say I want to go there someday, I really mean it. It's where my people are from. Only, I've never seen it. Kind of sad, really."

*Well, I'll see that you do see it. Someday. Somehow.*

After a bit more daydreaming, Darren suggested they eat their lunch. He climbed out of the plane first, then reached up to take Candy's hand as she stepped down. Her foot slipped on the top step, and she let out a small holler as she tumbled forward. . .directly into his arms. Talk about a happy disaster. They ended up face-to-face, just inches apart.

*Who's dreaming now?*

As he loosened her hold enough to let her feet touch down, she gasped. "I. . .I'm so sorry."

"I'm not." He kept his arms around her, enjoying the moment.

She looked up into his eyes. "I'm fine now, I promise. Thanks for catching me."

"My pleasure." He eventually released his hold completely but, after just a second apart, took her hands in his.

"Scared to let me go?" Candy gave him a sheepish look. "Afraid I'll fall again?"

"Something like that." Darren drew near. . .so near he could feel her breath on his cheek. He took a fingertip and traced her cheekbone. He could read the startled expression in her eyes at first, but it was soon replaced with a look of anticipation.

As he pulled her close, his heart rate seemed to pick up. He gave her a gentle kiss, first on one cheek, then the other. He paused to gaze into those gorgeous brown eyes.

Ironically, they now glistened with tears. "Are you all right?" he whispered.

"Yes, I. . ." She leaned her head against his chest. "Embarrassed, but. . .I'm very all right, actually." After a moment, she lifted her head and looked up at him, providing the perfect opportunity to kiss her. Never mind the fact that Jimmy's voice now rang out from behind him. Never mind that they stood in open view of half the airport. No, the only thing that mattered right now was the woman in his arms, the one he'd go on dreaming about for the rest of his life.

☙

Candy closed her eyes and enjoyed the unexpected kiss. It had come from out of the blue. She certainly hadn't planned to fall, let alone into Darren's arms. But being in his arms felt so right, so safe, she had to wonder why she hadn't fallen sooner.

Or maybe she had. Maybe she'd fallen some time ago and just not admitted it to herself. Surely he'd fallen, too, or his lips wouldn't be firmly locked onto hers. *Hmm.* In spite of her silliness in the plane, he obviously still found her grown-up enough to kiss.

And kiss again.

Her thoughts shifted in a dozen different directions at once, but she stopped them immediately. No point in thinking when one was kissing, right? And who cared that they were standing in a public place with people looking on?

After the second sweet kiss, Darren released her and the tips of his ears turned red. *I hear ya, mister.* Her cheeks felt like they were on fire.

"I don't know if I should apologize or throw a party." Darren gave her a sheepish look. "Did I. . .did I embarrass you?"

"Embarrass me?" She laughed. "I'm pretty good at doing that on my own, thank you very much."

He gave her an admiring look. Oh, how she wished she could read between the lines, to get into his head and figure out what he was thinking right now.

"You're good at a lot of things," Darren said.

"Like. . . ?"

"Like, bringing me out of my shell, for instance. And flying planes. And taking me places I've never been before. Places I didn't even know I wanted to see."

"It's just a little game I like to play."

She closed her eyes again and he whispered, "Tell me what you see now, Candy."

"I see. . ." She couldn't help but smile. "I see you."

He responded with a kiss that sent her heart soaring to the clouds.

# twelve

The next few weeks raced by. Before long, Candy found herself completely comfortable in the cockpit. She also found herself comfortable in Darren's arms. Their date in the Cessna 400 had been the perfect catalyst. Tumbling into his embrace might've been an accident, but it was the happiest one of her life. And talk about a great story! Who else could say their first kiss had happened while falling out of a plane? She couldn't have dreamed up such a happy tale.

Thankfully, Candy and Darren had plenty of time to explore their new relationship. Attending the same church helped. . .a lot. It gave them the perfect place to meet in a group setting. And, of course, they spent several off-duty hours hanging out with her roomies and Jason, too. Neither Candy nor Darren knew much about the Newark area, so they went from place to place, acting like silly tourists.

Before long, they settled into a comfortable routine. In fact, she could scarcely remember what life was like before Darren. Did she have a life before Darren? Funny, she couldn't picture it now.

More than anything, she looked forward to introducing him to her family. That dream would become a reality on August 19. . .the Saturday Jason and Brooke had chosen for the singles group outing to the boardwalk in Atlantic City. Till then, she would just have to be content sending pictures of Darren by e-mail and singing his praises to her sisters, who took the news with great zeal.

Unfortunately, not everything in Candy's life seemed to be moving in the same positive direction. As the days ticked by, tensions at Eastway grew, especially when another female pilot—Anna—was hired just three days after Darren's friend Gary received a second written warning.

By the second week in August, talks of union involvement had become more than a rumor. Even Darren, who rarely got worked up about anything, looked nervous. He occasionally shared his thoughts with Candy, but more often than not just shook his head whenever she asked him what the men were thinking of doing. Surely this would blow over in time.

In the midst of this turmoil, an idea occurred to Candy, one she couldn't seem to shake. She approached several of Eastway's female employees, hoping for their support. After a bit of corralling, a group of them met at DiMarco's on a Tuesday evening to implement a plan, one she'd dreamed up after some serious prayer on the matter.

After they had ordered their food, Candy broached the subject at hand. "So, here's what I'm thinking. Women have worked for the airlines for decades. Females in the industry... that's not a new thing. Not even close to new."

"Yeah, but our roles have sure changed," Shawneda said. She placed her glass back down on the table and gave Candy a pensive look. "It's not the coffee, tea, and me thing anymore. Flight attendants are taken more seriously. And most of the stereotypes are gone."

"Praise God for that." Brooke nibbled on a piece of garlic bread.

"A lot has changed...for sure," Candy said. "But the more I thought about this, the more I realized just how blessed we are that so many women walked this road ahead of us. They paved the way. You know?"

"I know I wouldn't be flying today if other women hadn't opened the doors for me." Anna nodded. "It's hard for us, but can you imagine how difficult it was for most of them? Back in the '30s and the '40s, when the industry was completely run by men?" She gestured for Brooke to hand over the loaf of garlic bread, which she did with a look of mock protest.

"We've come a long way," Candy agreed. "Especially in the last twenty years. And we have a lot to be thankful for." She took a sip of her diet soda and leaned back in her chair.

"Go on." Lilly gave her a curious look. "I have a feeling you're up to something."

"I am." Candy exhaled, working up the courage to continue. "This is what I'm thinking. What if we hosted a banquet honoring women who've made a real difference in aviation history? We could ask one of the women from the Ninety-Nines to come and speak. An older woman. Someone who's flown for years and has gained some notoriety for her achievements."

"Whoa." Brooke gave her an admiring look. "Do you really think we could pull that off? Get someone famous to come?"

"I guess we'll never know unless we ask. Right? And there are so many other women who were true pioneers in this industry. Some of the established members of Women in Aviation, for instance. What if we invited them to attend and honored them in some way? Then the men would see that women have a long-standing history in the aviation industry. And we could turn this whole thing into a fundraiser for scholarships."

"You don't think this would worsen the problems with the guys?" Lilly's wrinkled brow let Candy know how she felt about the idea. "I mean, they could just take this banquet as a sign we're trying to prove a point."

"Well, in some ways we are. But we're not trying to prove that women are better than men. Not at all." Candy grew more passionate about her subject matter as she continued. "I think we would be wrong to even attempt that. We're simply trying to prove that nothing has changed. We've been around in the industry for years. We're part of the past. . .and part of the future."

"So, how do we sell the guys on this idea?" Shawneda looked her way with a doubtful look in her eye.

"Why don't we enlist Darren?" Brooke suggested. "He's the perfect one to win over the other guys. He's more open-minded than most and he's a great communicator. Everyone respects him, too, and that's so important."

"I think that's a great idea." Lilly nodded. "He's so great at keeping people calm, and you're right. . .he's won the respect of both the men and the women."

"He's the perfect candidate, then." Brooke nodded. "And I'm pretty sure he's at the Eastway offices right now. Something about a meeting, I think. This would be just the right time to catch him and get his opinion."

"So, am I elected?" Candy looked at her friends.

"You're the best one to ask," Brooke assured her.

The food arrived and over steaming plates of lasagna and fettuccine, along with chilled Caesar salad, the women discussed ideas for the best possible banquet. By the time they finished, Candy had filled three tablet pages with notes. She could hardly wait to track down Darren to get his thoughts.

As soon as she ended her meal, Candy went up to the Eastway offices to find him. She ran into Marcella, one of the flight attendants, in the hallway. "Hey, I heard Darren was here in a meeting of some sort."

"Yeah, he's in a meeting of some sort." Marcella rolled her eyes. "With all the guys. But they wouldn't dare meet here. They're over in the small conference room at the Marriott."

"Oh?" Candy shrugged. "What kind of meeting?"

A strange look came over Marcella's face. "Candy, look. . . you're a great pilot and a wonderful girl. I don't like to be the one to tell you this, but the guys are all putting their heads together in preparation for Gary's meeting with union leaders tomorrow. Darren's right there with the other guys. . . in the thick of it."

"Oh, but he wouldn't—"

Marcella put her hands up in the air. "I can't read his mind, that's for sure. But he's in that meeting—not that you could call it a meeting, really. It's just a bunch of hot-headed guys blowing off steam. But if you don't believe me, go on over there and see for yourself."

"Okay." Candy wrestled with her thoughts, determined to give Darren the benefit of the doubt. "I'll go. But I know you're wrong. There's no way he would do that to me."

With determination settling in, she turned on her heels and headed for the Marriott.

❧

Darren sat in on the meeting in the familiar conference room, doing his best not to get involved. He'd come—not to link arms with Gary and the others, who'd simmered to the boiling point over the past few weeks—but to be a calming force. Unfortunately, he hadn't had a chance to get a word in edgewise, at least not yet.

Gary's face grew red as he spoke. "Eastway needs to be hiring based on skill and time in the air, not how pretty a pilot looks in her uniform."

Darren had to respond to that one. "Look, Gary, I think you're taking this a bit far. It's not a matter of getting more pretty faces onboard. These women are skilled pilots. I've flown with them and—"

"That's not all you've done with them." A snicker went up from the crowd after Gary's shocking statement. Darren felt his blood begin to boil. How dare they insinuate such a thing?

"For your information, my personal relationships are just that. . .personal. And I would never. . ." He wanted to finish the statement. Wanted to tell them he'd never cross lines of propriety with Candy in the way they had suggested. Wanted to tell them that a man of God guarded himself and the woman he cared for. Wanted to give them a piece of his mind. Instead, he drew in a deep breath and counted to ten, which opened the floor to one of the other disgruntled employees.

"Look," one of the pilots said. "This isn't about Darren or any other individual. It's simply about Eastway doing the right thing."

Darren struggled to keep from responding. Eastway didn't discriminate against men or women. Never had. From his point of view, the hirings and firings over the past few months had been based on performance. . .or the lack thereof. But how could he say so without hurting Gary and a couple of the others? If Eastway let them go, maybe they needed to go.

As he listened to the raised voices, Darren prayed. *Lord, I need Your perspective on this. If You want me involved, then You're going to have to really make it clear.*

Though he didn't agree with the arguments of the others, he couldn't help but feel he should play some role in calming the waters.

☙

Candy paced the hallway outside the conference room and prayed. She'd cracked the door and peeked inside but only saw the backs of the men's heads. Darren's voice hadn't been distinguishable from the others in the crowd, so she felt sure he wasn't in there. On the other hand, he wasn't answering his phone. Maybe he was home. . .sleeping. Catching a few z's before his next flight. Yes, that was surely it.

She turned to leave, but a rush from behind caused her to turn back. The conference room door flung open, and men began to flood toward her. *Yikes.* She'd never seen so many male Eastway employees in one place before. And talk about catching them at their worst. Several were using language she'd just as soon forget, and a couple were even spouting not-so-nice things about female pilots.

Until they saw her. One of them—Craig, the male flight attendant who'd always treated her kindly, at least to her face—took one look at her and turned the other way.

*Coward.*

A couple of the other men passed by with cold, hard

looks on their faces. . .cold enough to cause a shiver to run down her spine. Candy couldn't control whatever they were thinking or feeling. Only the Lord could do that.

She stood to the side of the hallway, waiting for the crowd to clear. Just one last peek in the room would do it. She would prove Marcella wrong. Darren couldn't possibly have supported these guys in their endeavors, particularly not with them so worked up.

The last of the men passed, and she breathed a sigh of relief. *See. I knew he wasn't here.*

Then she heard his voice. "Gary, you're my friend. You can count on me. You know I'd do anything for you." Darren slapped him on the back.

" 'Count on me'?" she whispered the words. "He's getting caught up in this now?" She ducked behind a large silk tree as Darren and Gary stepped out of the room, side by side. Thankfully, he never turned to look her way. And after today, she didn't know if she would ever turn his way again.

# thirteen

Candy managed to avoid a couple of calls from Darren in the days following his meeting with the men. She replayed his words in her mind several times over, trying to make sense of them: *"Gary, you're my friend. You can count on me. You know I'd do anything for you."*

How did this happen? Darren, of all people, knew Gary's record with the airline. Why not let the union officials take it from here? Why did he feel compelled to get involved. . .and on the men's side, no less?

Candy stewed over his sudden participation, but decided not to say anything about it, wondering if, instead, he would bring it up. Ironically, the two phone messages he'd left were completely unrelated to work. One had to do with an air show he was hoping they could attend together in a few weeks. The other had to do with the singles group trip to Atlantic City on Saturday. Candy didn't respond to either, unsure of what to say. Or do.

On Thursday morning, with plenty of free time ahead of her, she decided to take a walk to clear her mind. Maybe she could get some prayer time in along the way. She'd already poured her heart out to the Lord about all of this, but He seemed distant and quiet on the matter.

Though she and Darren had seen some of the sights in Newark, there were still so many places she had yet to discover. She'd heard the girls talk about Washington Park but had never seen it, except in passing. Today would be the perfect day to see things for herself. And to straighten out the troubling thoughts rolling through her mind.

Minutes later, Candy strolled the streets of the historic

district, taking in the sights. By the time she arrived at Washington Park, she'd already hashed out several of her more troubling questions with the Lord, questions like, "Whatever happened to all of that discernment I used to have?" and "When am I ever going to feel like an equal in this industry?"

Before long, she took a seat on a park bench, staring up at a statue of George Washington, mesmerized. Now, there was a man who'd stood up for what he believed in. A man who stuck to his guns, even when everything. . .and everyone. . . opposed him.

"Hmm." Things hadn't really changed all that much in the past two hundred years, had they?

Looking at the other statues, Candy's mind wandered. This whole place was filled with the memories of people who'd stood up for what they believed. Heroes who'd won the right. . . to live where they wanted, worship where they wanted, and work in occupations they loved. They'd sacrificed. . .and come out winners in the end.

"Lord, have You brought me here for a reason?"

Goose bumps covered her arms as she recognized the similarities to her situation. She began to pray. *Lord, I know You've called me to fly. I've known it since I was little. And I'm not ashamed of the fact that I'm doing what You called me to do. Help me overcome the fear of not being good enough. Take my insecurities and my worry about what people think. This isn't about what they think anyway, Father. It's about what You think. As long as I'm doing what You called me to do. . .*

Peace settled over her heart as she contemplated that fact. What was it Pop always said? *"The safest place to be is at the very center of God's will."* Storms could swirl around her, but in that safe place, she could move forward with confidence.

Still, there was that issue with Darren and the other men to iron out. Whenever she replayed the scene in her head, Candy could hardly believe it. Had Darren—the same man who'd kissed her that day at Essex County airfield—turned on her? Or was she just imagining it?

Every time his name flitted through her imagination, she saw those beautiful blue eyes. That dark wavy hair. She heard his voice. . .kind and yet authoritative. She saw his broad shoulders and the captain's bars on his sleeve. Every thought, every memory was a good one.

Still, all of the good things she knew of him faded away with the memory of his words: *"Gary, you're my friend. You can count on me. You know I'd do anything for you."*

*Ugh.* So much for trusting him. Now she couldn't even imagine spending time with him. How would she make it through the upcoming trip to Atlantic City with the singles group?

Candy cringed, thinking about going anywhere with him right now. Not with so many unspoken words between them. Still, how could she avoid the trip, especially when Jason and Brooke had gone out of their way to plan it with her in mind?

She rose from the bench and began to walk through the park, finally settling on a plan, one she felt sure everyone could live with. One that would give her the perfect opportunity to spend some time alone—to think and to pray.

Candy made the trek back to the apartment, then gathered her roomies together in the living room for an announcement.

"I, um. . .I've got several days off, so I think I'm going to head back home this evening."

"Home?" Lilly gave her a funny look. "You mean Atlantic City?"

"Yeah. I miss my family. And my younger sister, Tangie, is coming in from New York for her birthday. I really want to be there for that."

"But what about our trip to the boardwalk on Saturday?" Brooke's brow wrinkled. "You're not canceling, are you? I know Darren is really looking forward to meeting your family and seeing your old stomping ground. You're not going to let him down, are you?"

*Let* him *down?* Candy sighed. Maybe she should just come out and tell Brooke and the others what she'd overheard. Then they'd understand why she couldn't possibly spend a casual weekend with him. And they'd also see that he was the one letting her down, not the other way around.

On the other hand, why stir up a hornet's nest? The men were already worked up enough. Why get the women more involved than they already were?

"Candy, I haven't known you long, but I feel like we've been sisters forever." Brooke gave her a pensive look. "If you're going through some sort of problem with Darren—or anyone else, for that matter—don't run from it. You of all people have sticking power. Hang on and deal with it. That's what you'd tell me."

"I'm not running." She frowned. "It really is my sister's birthday. And I'm really going to Atlantic City to see my family." She paused, then added, "And I'm sure they'd be thrilled if you guys stopped by the candy shop for the party. It's going to be on Saturday night at eight, just after the store closes."

"Okay. Well, we'll be there. It'll be fun to see Ryan and Taffie again. And I wish I could talk you into joining us on the boardwalk for a couple of hours before that, but I understand if you want to be with your family."

"Yeah." Candy sighed. "I need to be around my sisters right now. Does that sound silly?"

"No." Lilly bit her lip before continuing. "But are you saying you might be thinking of quitting your job? 'Cause if you are. . ." Her voice trailed off.

"I don't know." Candy shrugged. "I don't like to see everyone so worked up. And based on the reactions of some of the guys, things aren't going to get any better for the female pilots. I sure don't enjoy working under this kind of stress."

"Well, forget about all that." Brooke gave her a sympathetic look. "Spend time with your sisters, and then we'll join you Saturday night. We'll put all of this other stuff out of our minds for now. How does that sound?"

"Amazing."

"I can't wait to meet your sisters." Shawneda grinned. "I have a feeling we're all going to be friends. If they're anything like you, I mean."

"Hmm." Candy couldn't help but smile as she thought about them. "To be honest, we're as different as night and day. Taffie's a homebody, always staying put. And Tangie. . ."

"What?" Lilly gave her a curious look.

"Well, she's going to be the next Broadway star. At least that's what she believes. And I don't doubt it. She's very at home on the stage. Performing."

"Wow. You are different, then," Shawneda said.

"Not so different, really." Brooke shrugged. "You just have a different stage to perform on. Yours is in the cockpit. But you're still the star of the show."

"I don't know about that."

"Well, you know what they say, 'The show must go on!' So, whatever you're struggling with, work through it with God, then get right back to the stage, okay?"

Candy sighed. "Okay. But in the meantime, just be praying for me, all right? I have a lot on my mind. A lot to work out."

"Will do."

Candy ventured off to her bedroom to pack. Surely a few days at home would do the trick. She hit the road by late afternoon, fighting traffic as she headed south on the Garden State Parkway. As she drove, she did her best to collect her thoughts and to focus on her family. Surely these next few days would help her put everything in perspective.

&

Late Thursday afternoon Darren tried one last time to call Candy. She'd avoided him for two days, but why? Had he done something—said something—to offend her? Had he somehow overlooked a birthday or forgotten a date? Not to his knowledge.

When she didn't answer the phone, he decided to give Jason a call. His best friend answered on the third ring with a jovial, "Hey, Darren. How are—"

"I blew it."

"Blew it? Blew what?"

"This thing with Candy." Darren paced the room. "I think I kind of. . .sort of. . ."

"What are you talking about? What have you done?"

"I have absolutely no idea."

Jason laughed. "Welcome to the world of male-female relationships. I'm not kidding when I say that half of the arguments Brooke and I have make no sense to me at all. Usually by the end of them I can't even remember how they got started."

"Well, we're not arguing. It's not like that."

"You're not? That's so strange, because Brooke just told me Candy had asked you to act as mediator in the Eastway dispute."

"Wait. . .really? 'Cause she never talked to me about that. In fact, she hasn't talked to me in days. And she won't answer my calls. Not a one. So, I've been thinking—"

"Well, that's your problem. You spend too much time doing that. Cut it out."

"Please. I might like to analyze things, but I don't usually overthink them." Darren exhaled, frustrated with the direction this conversation seemed to be going.

"Go ahead and believe that, if you like." Jason paused. "But maybe she just needs some space. Sometimes women are like that."

"Well, I've given her plenty of it. And actually, that's what I'm calling about. Trying to decide if I should give her even more."

"Oh?"

"I have a flight tomorrow," Darren explained, "but I'm still free on Saturday. Should I still go to Atlantic City with you guys, even if she doesn't go?"

"I think she's already there, actually."

"What?" *In Atlantic City? How come I'm the last to know this?*

"Brooke mentioned something about Candy driving down there tonight to see her family. I think she's staying till we get there."

"Really?" Darren brightened immediately. "So, maybe she's not avoiding me at all? Maybe she's just preoccupied with her family."

"That's likely." Jason laughed. "But don't worry. Remember, if this relationship with Candy is God's will, then any obstacles will be overcome in time. Even a deep thinker like yourself can't thwart God's plan. So, rest easy, okay?"

"I guess."

Darren ended the call and stared at the aquarium once more. No matter how many circles Fred made, he never actually went anywhere. Oh, he seemed content enough, but was it really enough, to get so settled in your ways you couldn't break free?

Darren approached the fish tank and dropped in a pinch of food. Fred swam up to the surface to grab it, then eventually went back to swimming around and around.

"Don't you ever just want to bust out of there?" Darren asked. "Swim in bigger ponds?"

Fred made the *Ooo* face again, then swam back down to his castle. Somehow the little guy had learned to be content with his circumstances, even without female companionship.

"I don't know, man." Darren sat on the sofa and stared at the fish tank. He watched as Fred swam in endless circles, going round and round the colorful castle in the center of the aquarium.

*Fred, I know just how you feel.*

## fourteen

Darren walked the boardwalk with Jason and Brooke, breathing in the salty air. The others in their group had stepped out ahead of them. A few headed over to the pier and a couple wanted to see a feature at the IMAX theater. Darren was content to stroll with no agenda in mind. It felt good to relax, to just be himself. To unwind. Leave the cares of the world—and Eastway—behind.

Of course, the crowd along the busy Atlantic City boardwalk proved problematic. And every few minutes another one of those rolling chairs came by, startling him. Interesting idea, folks being pushed around in wicker, canopied chairs-on-wheels. Still, he couldn't help but find the whole place. . . what was the word the women would use? Quaint? Yes, quaint.

"So, this is where Candy grew up." All of his talk about how much prettier the Pacific was than the Atlantic might have to be taken back. This was a great spot. And talk about attracting tourists. Umbrellas dotted the sand, and beachgoers toted their gear back and forth from the boardwalk to the water's edge.

Yes, this had a familiar feel to it. And with the scent of hot dogs and roasted peanuts in the air, he found himself drawn in.

"I'm getting hungry."

"Yeah, there's a great seafood place Ryan and Taffie told us about," Jason said. "Let's grab a bite to eat."

"Sounds good."

Minutes later they entered an eclectic fishy-smelling place with the words High Seas above the door. The décor was traditional coastal stuff, though Brooke was quick to warn him to use the word *shore* and not *coast*.

"What's the difference?" he asked with a shrug.

Brooke slapped herself in the head. "You're a California kid through and through, aren't you?"

"Well, yeah." No point in denying it.

Brooke rolled her eyes. "I don't expect you to understand. Just trust me on this. I grew up in Jersey, and around here, it's the shore."

As the waiter arrived at the table with their glasses of water, Darren turned to Brooke. "So, tell me what Candy said. She won't return my calls. And I don't have a clue what I've done."

"I don't know." Brooke shrugged, then took a sip of her water. "If she's upset with you, she's keeping it to herself. I just know she's been here in Atlantic City since Thursday, seeing her sister. And we're all invited to the party at the candy shop tonight."

"Why don't we head over there now when we're done eating? I want to see her." He glanced at his watch. Three fifteen. Hmm. A little early.

"Darren, just give her some space. She obviously wants it. I'm sure it's all going to be clearer before long, but not if you push too hard."

"Sounds just like what I told him." Jason looked up from his menu. "One thing I've learned about women. When they need their space, they need their space. There's no crowding them. And you'll do more damage than good if you push things."

"I guess." He shrugged. "And it's not that I feel like pushing. I just need to know that she's okay, that I haven't upset her in some way." He turned to Brooke. "Surely she would tell you if she was upset with me, right?"

"Darren, I've only known Candy a couple of months. She's different from most of the others in our apartment. And even though she's opened up to me about a lot of things, she hasn't mentioned anything specific about her relationship with you. Not lately, anyway."

"Not lately?"

"Well, I heard every detail of how she fell out of the plane into your arms, and how you kissed her on the fly." A grin slowly spread across Brooke's face as she repeated, "On the fly. Hey, that's pretty good. But anyway, that's old news."

"But you two are definitely an item, right?" Jason gave him an inquisitive look. "Sure seems that way."

"I thought so."

"And whatever happened with Andrea?" Brooke asked.

"I got another call from her a few days ago." He sighed. "She's coming back in town this weekend and wants to get together. I don't want to hurt her feelings, but I just don't feel right about it. Even though Candy and I aren't officially a couple, my heart is certainly. . .involved."

"Just tell Andrea you're seeing someone else." Jason shrugged. "She'll get it."

"Yeah." He paused a moment. "I'm just worried because I'm not actually 'seeing' someone else at the moment. I can't even get Candy to respond to me."

"Time and space." Jason repeated the words, then glanced at his watch. "Let's get your mind off of women after we eat. Want to play some Skee-Ball?"

"Waste of money." Darren leaned back in his chair, defeated. No point in playing games without Candy around.

"What's the problem with spending a few bucks on a little harmless fun? I'm not asking you to gamble it away, after all. What've you got to lose?"

*Yeah. What've I got to lose?* After all, the only thing he'd lost so far. . .was his heart.

❧

Candy spent her afternoon at her parents' house, chatting with Tangie. She felt a little guilty letting Taffie and Ryan handle things at the shop without her, but they'd insisted. When the clock in the living room struck six, their mother called out from the kitchen.

"Okay, you two. We're leaving in fifteen minutes for the shop to set up for the party."

"How many people are coming, Mom?" Candy asked as she rose from the sofa.

Her mother rounded the corner into the living room to join them. "I'm thinking probably forty or more." She paused to dry her hands on the dishcloth she was holding. "All of Tangie's closest friends from high school will be there, and half the kids who were in the youth group with you girls. 'Course I guess they're not kids anymore. They're all twenty-somethings."

"Yes, but it'll make us feel like kids again." Tangie's eyes sparkled with delight.

"You *are* a kid." Candy sighed as she looked at her very eclectic-looking younger sister. The shocking red orange hair always took people by surprise. So did the pierced nose. But underneath that colorful exterior lay a heart of gold, one that was often overlooked by folks who refused to dig deeper than the physical.

"So, do you think Corey Lutton's going to be there tonight?" Tangie waggled her brows. "He always had such a crush on you when we were kids. And I hear his fiancée just broke his heart a few months ago, so he's available. Might help you through the heartbreak over you-know-who."

" 'You-know-who'?" Their mother put her hands up in mock despair. "Is there something you need to tell me?"

"Well, I. . ."

"Did you meet someone while Pop and I were off RVing? Why am I always the last to know?"

Candy shrugged, feeling conflicted. "I don't know. I mean, I was seeing someone, but now he's. . ."

"He's what?" Tangie's eyes widened, showing off her heavy eyeliner. "Married to someone else? In a coma? Incapacitated in some way? C'mon, Candy. Why don't you just tell us what happened between you and Darren?"

"Darren?" Their mother looked back and forth between them. "His name is Darren? The one who broke your heart?"

Could this get any worse? "Well, he didn't really break my heart. He doesn't even know that I know. . .oh, never mind." Candy groaned.

"I'm so out of the loop," Candy's mother said with a look of exaggerated despair. "I guess that's what happens when your kids grow up. The mother is replaced by sisters and friends. No one ever calls. No one ever writes. . . ." Her voice drifted off and she sighed. Loudly.

"No, Mom." Candy laughed. "I could never replace you. And Darren didn't really break my heart. We've just. . .well, something's happened and I had to step back."

"Oh. . ." Tangie's mouth stayed in the perfect *O* position for a moment before she whispered, "Were you two getting too close, too fast?"

Their mother paled and excused herself to the kitchen.

"No. Nothing like that." Candy gave her sister a friendly punch in the arm. "You know me better than that. I have every intention of staying pure until I'm married."

"Right. But sometimes people slip up, especially when they're in love."

*In love? Am I in love with Darren?*

"So, what happened?" Tangie asked. "Why did you back off?"

"You're just going to have to trust me when I say it's for the best. I have a few things to figure out. And I think Darren does, too."

"Darren. I still can't get over that name." Tangie wrinkled her nose. "Not very romantic."

"Don't even get me started on names." *Not when I've been "Cotton Candy" all my life.* She took a couple of steps toward the hallway. "I've got to get dressed so we can leave. What about you?"

"What's wrong with what I'm wearing?" Tangie gestured at her mismatched shorts and T-shirt, then added, "Kidding.

Kidding." She padded along behind Candy, whispering, "Hey, while you're figuring this out, take another look at Corey Lutton, okay? 'Cause if you don't, I just might."

Candy laughed. "You go right ahead. Won't bother me a bit."

Tangie shrugged. "His mother never liked my tattoos or my hair. I think she's looking for a different kind of girl for her son."

"And I'm that girl?"

Tangie grinned. "Well, I have it on good authority you're pretty high on the list."

A groan escaped Candy's lips. "Stop it, Tangie. No match-making. Not tonight."

"Who, me? This time it's Mom and Mrs. Lutton conspiring against you. Or for you. Or, whatever you call it."

"I call it unnecessary."

"Well, to Mom's credit, she didn't know about Darren. I can't believe you never told her, by the way."

"I was actually going to tell her tonight. He's coming to the party with Jason and Brooke and a few others from our singles group, so I'm going to have to explain. And besides, he doesn't know I'm—"

"Wait. He doesn't know you're upset with him?" Tangie's eyes widened. "Man, this is going to be great. Better than a soap opera. Corey and Darren in the same room. Darren not knowing you're dumping him because of. . .why are you dumping him again? Anyway, I'm getting dressed in a hurry. Don't want to miss a thing."

Candy sighed, then walked into her room and closed the door. As she changed for the party, she thought about Darren. *Why? Why is he pretending to be interested in me, then going behind my back to help the men? Is he using me? Have they put him up to this?*

The more she thought about it, the more her skin began to crawl. It did make sense. All of that getting-to-know-you stuff at Essex County airport could just as easily have been a ruse. . .a way to get her to open up and talk. Thank goodness she'd kept her thoughts about Eastway to herself that day.

On the other hand, she'd acted like a silly kid in the cockpit of the Cessna 400, hadn't she? And her childishness had surely given Darren and the other men plenty of fodder. By now they probably all thought her to be immature, at best.

Fully dressed, she paused to check her reflection in the mirror above her childhood dresser—the same mirror that she'd stared into hundreds, if not thousands, of times as a teen. "Mirror, mirror on the wall. . ." She mouthed the words, "Who's the most naive of all?"

Only one name came to mind.

Candy exhaled loudly. Perhaps she'd been naive up till now, but no more. Staring into her reflection, she made up her mind, once and for all. Pop had been right. All of that head-in-the-clouds stuff. And look where it had gotten her. Her daydream mentality had landed her squarely in the middle of a controversy at Eastway.

Well, no more. From this point on, she'd guard her every move. No more being taken advantage of. She would put away childish things once and for all.

# fifteen

Darren's anticipation grew as the hours ticked by. He'd seen enough of the boardwalk, already. Played enough games. Nearly been run over by those goofy chairs half a dozen times at least. Listened to kids screaming and parents scolding. Eaten fried fish. Couldn't they just get on with it?

Finally, around 7:40 p.m., he managed to convince Brooke and Jason they should go to the candy shop. Who cared if they were a little early for the party? He wanted to see Candy. And surely she wanted to see him...in spite of the unanswered calls.

At exactly 7:43, Darren, Brooke, Jason, and the others from the singles group stood in front of the colorful candy shop.

"Wow." So this is where she grew up. The playfulness of the place fit right in with her girlish charm. He looked up at the sign above the door. Beneath the words CARINI'S CONFECTIONS they'd placed a scripture from Psalm 119:103: HOW SWEET ARE YOUR WORDS TO MY TASTE, SWEETER THAN HONEY TO MY MOUTH! Clever.

"You ready?" Jason slapped him on the back.

"Like we could stop him." Brooke rolled her eyes, then turned to the others in the group. "He's been begging us for hours to bring him here."

Darren's heartbeat escalated as he looked back at the sign. Looked like he was about to meet Candy's family face-to-face. And the idea of seeing her again...especially on her own turf... put knots in his stomach. *Why can't things just be easy?*

He followed along behind Jason as they entered the crowded shop. Darren looked around in awe. "Wow. I've never seen anything like this." The right side of the shop was dedicated to candies. And talk about color! He stared in awe at the rows and rows of sweets. Everything from large glass jars of saltwater taffy to caramel apples to rock candy. And the smell! A distinct sugary sweetness hung in the air, one that put him in mind of his childhood.

He looked to his left, taking in the trendy coffee bar. Looked—and smelled—very tempting. And the old-fashioned ice cream area put him in mind of something from the turn of the century. The whole place amazed him. People of any and every age would feel at home here.

Others in the group scattered to various places in the store. . . most of the women heading over to purchase taffy and other candy products. Darren worked his way through the crowd, almost losing sight of Jason and Brooke. They finally arrived at the coffee counter where Brooke squealed with delight.

"Ryan!" She quickly made introductions. "Guys, this is my cousin, Ryan Antonelli. Ryan, you know Jason." When the dark-haired stranger nodded, Brooke added, "And this is our friend, Darren."

"Darren, good to meet you." He extended his hand. "Let me see if I can find my wife. She's going to be so glad you're here."

Minutes later, Darren stood in front of an unfamiliar woman, slightly older than Candy, yet resembling her in every conceivable way. "Wow. You must be Taffie."

"My fame precedes me." She laughed. "How did you know that?"

"Oh, your sister Candy. She and I are. . ." He wasn't sure how to finish the sentence. If someone had asked him a couple of weeks before, he would've said "dating." No problem. But, now? When she wouldn't even answer his calls. . .

"Oh, I remember now." Taffie's face lit up. "You're the guy in the pictures."

"Pictures?"

Taffie nodded. "Candy sent pictures of you a couple of weeks ago. There was one of you standing next to a small plane. I think the caption said something about Big Ben. Or the English countryside. Maybe both."

*Okay, well, that's embarrassing.* Still, it gave him hope. If Candy had told her sister about their date, maybe her silence of late was simply a coincidence.

"Candy just got here," Taffie said. "She's with my mom and Tangie back in the office. They're dealing with decorations. We're about to close the shop to the public and set things up for the party. You're just in time to help."

"Help decorate?" *Is she kidding?*

"Why not?" Brooke nudged him, then whispered, "You want to make a good impression on the family, right? Well, here's your chance."

Taffie put him to work filling balloons at the helium tank. With his attention more on the back of the room than the task at hand, he sent a couple of balloons sailing off across the room.

"He can fly a plane *and* a balloon," Brooke teased.

"Here, let me do that." Ryan took over. "You're a guest, after all."

Darren nodded and muttered an apology, all the while keeping his gaze on the back of the room. His heart could hardly stand the wait.

Thankfully, a couple of minutes later, Candy emerged with an older woman on one side and a younger woman on the other. *Okay, that's her mom. Typical Italian mama with salt and pepper hair—more salt than pepper. And that's got to be Tangie. The piercings and tattoos are a dead giveaway. And the orange hair. Couldn't miss that if I wanted to.*

Darren's attention shifted at once to Candy. The moment their eyes locked, her expression changed—from joy to one of concern, then. . .something else. He couldn't quite place it, but she didn't exactly look happy to see him.

"Candy!" Brooke grabbed her and gave her a hug. "Darren could hardly wait to get here. Hope you don't mind that we're early."

Tangie's brow wrinkled. She appeared to be sizing him up. "So, you're Darren."

"I'm Darren."

"Mm-hmm." She stared a bit longer, then turned to her sister. "He's handsome, Candy. A lot more handsome in person than in the pictures you sent."

Darren felt the heat rise to his cheeks at her words. On the other hand, this might just work to his advantage. If he could win over the sisters, surely any fences could be mended.

"I'm not sure Corey's going to stand a chance next to this guy." Tangie nudged Candy with her elbow.

*Corey?* Okay, that changed everything.

Candy's cheeks reddened, and she mumbled something about decorating the cake.

"So, you're Darren." Her mother gave him a suspicious look as if to ask, *"What have you done to hurt my daughter?"*

"I. . .I'm Darren." He extended his hand in her father's direction.

The older man appeared to be oblivious to any problems. He shook Darren's hand and offered a warm smile. "Nice to meet you. We're glad you could come." He gestured around the room. "All of you."

"It's great to finally meet you, too. I've looked forward to this day for ages." Darren stumbled his way into a rehearsed speech about how much he'd enjoyed getting to know Candy, and how he'd wanted to meet her parents ever since their first date. "As a Christian, it's just so important to me to have a good relationship with the whole family, not just the girl I'm dating."

" 'The girl I'm dating.' " Mrs. Carini drew in a deep breath and shook her head. "Strange. Just so strange." She turned back toward the ice cream counter, and Candy followed on her heels. Darren watched it all in a state of confusion. What in the world had he done to upset everyone. . .and how could he possibly undo it?

Candy's heart raced as she followed on her mother's heels. When they reached the area behind the ice cream counter, her mom opened the freezer door and hid behind it.

"Tell me again why I'm not supposed to like this guy?" she whispered. "He's great. Sounds like he's a strong Christian. . . handsome, too. And he's clearly head over heels for you."

"I know, but. . ." Candy couldn't think of anything else to say. Not now. Why ruin her sister's big night? Besides, her mother didn't need to know that Darren's kindness was possibly just an act. That he'd gone behind her back to. . .

*Hmm. To do what?* She still hadn't really figured all of that out yet.

Her mother handed her the ice cream cake. With a shaky hand, Candy wrote, Happy 21ST, Tangie! on top. Her hand trembled so much the words were barely distinguishable.

Taffie approached. She glanced down at the cake and said, "Wow. Hmm." They both continued to stare at the sloppy script for a moment.

"I know." Candy sighed. "I don't know what's wrong with me."

"No problem. I'll just scrape that off and rewrite it. Won't hurt your feelings, will it?"

"No. Won't hurt my feelings."

Funny. At the words "hurt my feelings," her gaze shifted to Darren. Standing there, chatting with her parents and Ryan, he looked to fit right in. She could see him merging into the Carini clan with little effort, especially after his impassioned speech about falling in love with the whole family.

If only they didn't have that one obstacle to overcome. . . the one where he had turned on her behind her back.

Determined to focus on other things, she went to work helping Ryan fill helium balloons, then place them around the shop. She sighed with relief as the bell jangled. Good. Party guests. That would provide a nice distraction.

Or not.

She looked over into the anxious eyes of Corey Lutton and his parents. *Oh no.* Corey looked at her with a hopeful expression, then walked her way for a hug. Every eye in the place looked their way as Corey's strong arms wrapped her in a slightly-too-long embrace. In that moment, she contemplated taking ten or twelve of the helium balloons. . . tying them together. . .and soaring off over the Atlantic.

Instead, she returned Corey's hug, welcomed his family, then went to work. . .pretending everything was all right.

## sixteen

Darren managed to make it through the party, but not in the best frame of mind. Candy had avoided him all night, even going so far as to sit with that Corey fellow and his parents during the party, but no more. He would get to the bottom of this if it killed him. And it just might.

He approached her just as the others were beginning to leave. "Candy?"

She turned his way with a cautious look on her face. "Yes?"

"We need to talk." Darren didn't mean for his words to come across sounding gruff, but they did.

Candy sighed before answering. "Yes, I know. We do." Without so much as a word, she set off toward the door.

Darren followed along behind her until they stood outside the shop on the boardwalk. She then took several rapid steps, moving them farther away from the store. *Where are you going?*

"Candy, slow down."

When she turned to him, he noticed tears in her eyes. "Wait. Why are you crying? What in the world is happening here? Has someone done something to hurt you?"

Pain registered in her eyes immediately. "Darren. . ." She seemed to be grasping for words. "I told you that day at Essex County that I've always been a dreamer. Always had big ideas."

"Right." He shrugged. *What does this have to do with anything?*

"I need you to know that I've worked really hard to get to the place I'm at."

"Well, I can certainly appreciate that. I've done the same."

A tear spilled over her lashes and she brushed it away. "I've spent nearly two years away from my family. . .getting my wings. Building time. Taking the job in Newark. It's been a huge sacrifice."

"I know. I never said—"

A large group passed by them, laughing and talking loudly.

Candy put her hand up to stop him from continuing. "I'm just saying that I didn't just decide one day I wanted to fly. I've poured every ounce of strength into making this dream a reality, and I've prayed about it every step of the way. Every door that's opened has been opened by God. Yes, my dreams are big, but they're mine. And I'm not going to let anyone shoot them down."

"Shoot them down?" He paused, completely dumbfounded. What did this have to do with him? "Are you talking about the guys? 'Cause if you are, you need to know that—"

"I'm talking about you." She faced him dead-on and looked him squarely in the eye.

"W–what?"

"I'm talking about you going behind my back to meet with the men. Making promises to help them try to bring me down. Supporting them behind my back."

"Bring you down?" He shook his head, confused. "Wait a minute, Candy. There's been some kind of misunderstanding here."

"So, you can honestly stand there and tell me you're not working with the guys?"

"Working with them?" He stared at her, completely stunned. "What makes you think that? I'm certainly not in favor of what they're doing, if that's what you think." Could she really think that of him? If so, how could he possibly convince her otherwise?

⁂

Shame washed over Candy as she stared into Darren's pain-filled eyes. "So, that day at the Marriott. . ."

"Day at the Marriott?" Wrinkles formed between his eyes

for a second, then his eyes widened. "Candy. . .you were at the Marriott on the day the men met?"

She nodded, feeling the lump rise in her throat. "I was."

"I never saw you."

"I was, um, hiding behind a tree."

Darren laughed. "Well, why didn't you make your presence known?" Just as quickly he caught himself. "No, never mind. I get it. The men weren't in the best frame of mind. But when you saw me, why didn't you say something? Jump out from behind the tree? Give me a piece of your mind? If you thought I was—"

"I don't know." She groaned. "I saw you patting Gary on the back and telling him that you would support him. . . ."

"Ah, I get it. You thought I meant support him in the cause?" Darren shook his head. "No, I was talking about something else entirely. He'd just told me about a possible job offer with a charter service in Philly. I'd told him I'd support him in prayer. Told him I was onboard to pray for favor for the new job."

"Oh no." She groaned again, more than a little ashamed for her assumptions.

"He's my friend. And even though he's had some problems, I still care about him. He's got an attitude, but he's a good pilot. A little time working for less money will do him some good. But did you really think. . .?" Darren's voice trailed off.

Candy sighed and shook her head. "How did I do this? How did I mess this up so royally?"

"You didn't. It's just a misunderstanding."

"But that's just it. I'm tired of misunderstandings. I'm tired of the junior-high problems in a grown-up world. I've always been accused of being flighty. And I can't act like a grown woman, even when I try."

"Oh, you're wrong about that." He drew near and her arms instinctively wrapped around his waist as he pulled her close. Anticipation washed over Candy, along with pure joy. "You're a very grown-up woman, Candy Carini. Plenty grown-up for me." He kissed the end of her nose and she felt every anxiety lift. Funny how just one kiss could do that. It spoke a thousand words. No, a hundred thousand.

His lips met hers for a gentle kiss. Well, gentle at first. After a moment, the intensity of the moment seemed to sweep over them both. Darren backed up and smiled at her. "I think we've just proven you're not a little girl. But I think we'd better stop while we're ahead. You might be a little *too* much woman for me."

Candy felt her cheeks warm. "Somehow I doubt that. But you're right. I'm just so...so happy right now."

"Me, too." He pulled her close and kissed her forehead. "Now, we've got to promise we'll always talk things through. No more avoiding, okay?"

"Okay." She sighed, but inwardly rejoiced. Something about his use of the word *always* gave her such hope.

❧

Though the crowd of people pressed in around him, Darren felt like he and Candy had slipped off into their own private world. Had she really thought he would turn on her? He could never do that. Still, with the little she'd overheard at the Marriott, her reactions now made sense.

"Candy, I have to tell you something."

She looked up at him with a hopeful expression.

"These past few days have been awful. Just being away from you for that length of time almost did me in. My heart is..." He pushed beyond the lump in his throat to continue. "My heart is completely..."

"What?"

"It's not mine anymore." He smiled as the words settled into his spirit. "Ugh. I'm not saying this right."

"No, you're doing fine," she said.

"What I'm trying to say...what I need to say...is, I love you."

Her eyes filled with tears. "Do you mean that?"

"Of course." He planted kisses in her hair. "And don't ever doubt it."

"I won't." She rested comfortably in his embrace as the reality of her feelings became clear, then whispered, "You know I love you, too, right?"

"Mm-hmm."

Nothing else needed to be said for a few moments. Darren finally broke the silence. "I'm going to do my best to keep the lines of communication wide open from now on. And as far as the men at Eastway go, well, I'm going to do my best to put them in their place. You're too good a pilot to take the kind of flack they've dished out. And you're too good a woman. . ." Here he stumbled over the words, "to ever have to deal with unnecessary pain."

"Thank you." Her eyes brimmed over.

"Sorry. I didn't mean to make you cry."

"Oh, I'm not sad." A girlish giggle escaped. "Sometimes I just get emotional when I'm happy. And right now, I'm very, very happy."

"Me, too."

He wrapped her in his arms for a final embrace. Funny, standing here on the boardwalk with people passing by, there were no problems left for the two of them to solve. And if life did happen to toss them any unexpected challenges. . . with God's help, they would soar above them.

## seventeen

In the days following his trip to Atlantic City, Darren found himself on a proverbial roller-coaster ride. Every time he thought about Candy. . .about their conversation and the kiss that followed, he wanted to shout for joy. Then, just about the time he started to do so, something at Eastway would come along to bring him down, if only for a moment.

One major complication had arisen. In spite of Gary's meetings with union officials, Eastway carried through with its threats and fired him. No issues of sexism from the airline could be proven, nor should they, at least to Darren's way of thinking. Gary had made his mistakes when he demeaned his crew and now paid a hefty price. This had nothing to do with the hiring or firing of anyone else. Still, there remained an undercurrent of discontentment among the men, and Darren made it a priority to pray about the situation every day.

He prayed about something else, too, something hidden deep in his heart that he hadn't shared with anyone—an idea that had been formulating for some time now. One that could very well change the course of his life, if he made the right move at the right time. If the Lord would give him the go-ahead, Darren just might find himself soaring in a completely new and different direction.

But first, he would have to get a rock-solid answer from on high. No point in flying off on a tangent without asking the Lord His opinion first.

Oh, but if only the heavens would open up and rain down his answer. Then Darren Furst would be the happiest of men.

Not that he wasn't happy already. These days, he found himself cracking more jokes than ever, and waiting for every opportunity to make people smile. Joy flooded his heart, particularly when he spent time with Candy. And he finally found himself free to dream again. . .really dream. She had that effect on him, to be sure.

There were other changes, as well. With Jason's help, Darren spent some time talking through the problems he'd faced because of the poor interaction between his parents. Maybe, with time, he could develop a better relationship with them. Of course, it might require a trip to San Diego, but he could manage that.

In the meantime, there was plenty to take care of in Newark. Candy and her friends were all abuzz about an upcoming banquet they were hosting. Hopefully it would be just the ticket. . .just the thing to bring the men and women of Eastway together.

※

Candy returned to Newark with renewed joy and peace in her heart. Despite Gary's firing, she knew it had nothing to do with her hiring. . .or anyone else's for that matter. So, in spite of any communication issues with the men—or lack thereof— she decided to move forward with the banquet featuring prominent women in aviation.

With Brooke, Anna, and Shawneda in tow, she selected the perfect spot—the Dorothy Ball House at Lincoln Park. All around the park stood brownstone mansions, built in the mid-nineteenth century. . .homes of the elite of the day. In that place, so rich with history, they would celebrate the achievements of women from the past, the present, and the future.

Candy had managed to secure two speakers for the evening, an elderly woman named Margaret Franklin, age seventy-nine. She'd flown a medic plane during the Vietnam War and agreed to speak on the topic, "The Changing Role of Women in Aviation." And then there was Norah Bonner, the youngest woman working for a commercial airline. Funny, how close

Candy came to winning that prize herself. Norah agreed to share her story of how she came to fly.

On the first Saturday in September, Candy met with the other women from Eastway at the banquet site to finalize plans. They walked through the various rooms of the facility, finally stopping in the banquet room. Once there, they paused and looked around.

"How many people are we expecting again?" Shawneda asked with a dubious look on her face.

"At last count, one hundred twenty. Maybe a few more." Candy reached for her clipboard, flipping pages until she found the one she was looking for. "Yes. One-twenty. More or less."

"Hope it's less." Shawneda pursed her lips as she reexamined the room.

"I've got a couple of RSVPs still to come." Candy shrugged. "But I'm sure this will all work out."

"Hope you're right. I don't know how we're going to fit that many people in here." Brooke looked doubtful.

Candy sighed. "We have no choice. But how did I know so many of the women would respond? We've got ladies coming from five different states. I couldn't fathom there would be such an amazing turnout. But it's such a great thing. The money we raise will go for scholarships for incoming female pilots."

"I don't know if I ever told you, but I got a scholarship when I first started flight school," Anna said. "It helped a lot. I could never have paid for it on my own, and I know my parents couldn't have, either."

Shawneda sighed and dropped into a nearby chair.

"What's wrong?" Candy looked her way, puzzled by her friend's reaction.

"You're just bringing up old memories. I wanted to. . ."

"What?" All of the women gathered around her.

Shawneda's eyes brimmed over with tears. "You all see me as this happy-go-lucky flight attendant, and for the most part

I am. But you don't know that I really wanted to go to flight school. My parents got divorced when I was in high school, so just about the time I really started thinking about it, well. . ."

"Oh, I never knew." Brooke knelt down next to her. "Why didn't you tell me?"

Shawneda shrugged. "I don't know. I guess I didn't want to get into the whole story about my family's lack of finances. And trust me, just the idea of taking out loans to go to flight school was out of the question. So, I went the other route. And don't get me wrong, being a flight attendant is great, but. . ."

"It's not too late." Anna pulled up a chair next to her. "Maybe some of the scholarship money could be used for you."

"Oh, no. I wasn't implying anything like that." Shawneda looked stunned at first, and then embarrassed. "Just hearing about it made me a little. . .reminiscent. Besides, it's all water under the bridge now. The past is in the past. You know?"

"Well, yes," Candy agreed. "But the purpose of this banquet is to celebrate where we are today. . .and where we're heading. So, if I were you, I'd be praying about this, Shawneda. Seriously. Because God just might open a door. I happen to know of a great flight school on Long Island. You could get your training there." She put her clipboard down, sat down, and went into a lengthy explanation of what it would take for Shawneda to get her license.

By the time their conversation ended, nearly twenty minutes had passed. Candy and the others prayed with Shawneda—right there in the Dorothy House—about her secret desire to fly. Candy knew from her own experience that the desire usually didn't go away on its own. No, most of the people who had the bug ended up flying. . .sooner or later. The more Candy thought about it, the more excited she got. Perhaps, with some of the event's incoming scholarship money, she could play a role in helping her roomie fulfill a lifelong dream.

They wrapped up their prayer time just as a familiar voice rang out. "Are we having church?"

"Darren!" She rose and rushed his direction. "What are you doing here?"

"Well, a little bird told me you'd be here. I thought maybe you might let me take you to dinner. Are you hungry?"

"Am I ever! But can you give us a few more minutes to wrap up? We were just about to shift gears and talk about decorations."

"Woo-hoo. It's my lucky night. One lone man in a banquet room with four women talking about decorations."

"Hey now." She gave him a pouting look. "We want this night to be a rousing success and half the fun is the decorating." She turned to the others, excitement growing. Reaching for her clipboard once again, she read some things she'd written down. "We're going with a fairly simple theme with great fall colors. I've come up with a fun idea for centerpieces for the table, but I need someone to make them." Her gaze shifted to Darren, who'd taken to cleaning his nails.

After a moment's pause, he looked up. "What? Who, me?"

"Yes, you and Jason and maybe some of the other guys. We need model airplanes."

"Oh, that's easy. I've got at least five or six at my place."

"I know. But we're going to have fifteen tables at least," she explained. "And then the head table for the speakers and their husbands. So, we're probably talking at least twenty model airplanes. Planes from all different eras, I mean. And wouldn't it be cool to have several hanging up, too?"

"Twenty?" Darren shook his head. "Do you have any idea how long it takes to put together even one? It's tedious work."

Candy sighed. "Well, maybe if we check around we'll find a few more already made. But let's go to the hobby shop this afternoon, Darren. Okay? Before we eat?"

He shrugged. "Sure. Why not. When is this shindig again?" He raked his fingertips through his now-messy hair. "I might have to hire outside help."

"It's the last Saturday of this month, so you have three weeks."

"Three weeks." He whistled. "Man. You don't know what you're asking."

"Oh, and tell me what you think about this." Candy turned back to her friends. "I'm thinking we can elevate the model planes in the center of each table. . .maybe on a small box. And we'll cover each box with polyfill to look like clouds."

"Too cool." Brooke nodded.

Anna added an affirmative, "I like it."

They wrapped up the rest of their plans, focusing primarily on the menu, then Candy turned to Darren. "Ready to go shopping?"

"My favorite question." He grinned. "I'm fine with it. Just don't take me to the mall or make me watch you pick out shoes for this big event, okay? I have my limits." He winked at her and she laughed in response.

"Oh, you just reminded me, I do need to get some new shoes. And a new dress, too."

The women dove into an animated conversation about their attire for the banquet, and Darren sighed. Candy knew he wasn't really frustrated. He was used to hanging around the women, after all. He knew how they were. And he never seemed to mind.

Still, as they went on and on about evening gowns versus party dresses, she did notice when he began making his way to the door. He mouthed, "I'll be waiting outside," and she nodded. Hopefully she wouldn't keep him waiting long.

❧

Darren heard his cell phone ring and reached to answer it. He glanced down at the phone, stunned to see a familiar number with a 619 area code displayed.

"Mom?" He spoke the word hesitantly.

"Darren, it's Dad. I'm using your mother's cell phone. She's. . ."

"What, Dad?"

"We're at the hospital. She's having a little procedure done."

"Procedure? What kind?"

"Well. . ." He paused long enough for fear to kick in. "Some sort of thing where they put dye into your arteries so they show up on an x-ray. I think they called it a. . ." He paused again. "Hang on, son. Let me look at this paper they gave me. Oh, okay. It's called a cardiac catheterization."

"Wait." Darren allowed the words to register. "Are you saying that Mom has a heart problem?"

"Well, they're not sure yet. But she had a little spell a few days ago. Wasn't the first one."

"Dad, you should've called me."

"She didn't want me to. You know how stubborn your mom can be."

"Yes, but I still need to know these things so I can be praying."

"Well, she's been through a lot of stress at work over the past few weeks, so I was hoping they'd come back and say she was just having an anxiety attack or something like that, but the cardiologist said it might be something else. So they're doing this procedure."

Darren shuffled the phone to his other ear. "Is this some sort of surgery?"

"Not really. And she's wide awake. They're putting a catheter through an artery in her leg and somehow leading it up to her heart. Then they put the dye in."

"She's awake? Why aren't you in there with her?"

Another sigh from his father let him know exactly why. "She wouldn't let me. You know how she is."

"Stubborn." They repeated the word in unison.

"Your mother's got a mind of her own." His dad sounded weary. "And heaven knows I've tried to get her to slow down. She works too hard. And she's always anxious or upset about something. Her blood pressure's been running on the high side, but the doctor said that's probably a result of stress. The lawyer she works for is representing some guy in a high-profile case, and she's been up to her ears in paperwork as they prepare for trial."

Darren shook his head, unable to figure out what to say next. His mother had always been high-stress. Always in command. Always demanding and bossing others around, even at the law firm where she worked. No doubt her body had finally started to react. No one could keep up that kind of pressure without eventual problems.

"Dad, I know you don't want to hear this," he finally worked up the courage to say, "but you're going to have to get Mom to listen to you. She's got to follow the doctor's orders and slow down. Stay calm."

"Humph."

"I know. But. . ." Darren sighed. "Let's just pray about this. And in the meantime, I'll be praying for the results of this test. Keep me posted, okay?"

"I will." Another hesitation followed, then, "Son?"

"Yes, Dad?"

"I love you. And we miss you. Wish you'd come for a visit."

"I will, Dad. Especially if you need me."

They ended the call, and Darren gripped the phone in his hands. At that moment, Candy and the others emerged from the building, still chirping like baby birds as they talked about the banquet. His father's news still gripped his heart.

Candy looked over at Darren, her brow wrinkled in concern. "Darren? What's happened?"

"My mom." He shook his head. "She's been having some heart problems. That was my dad on the phone."

"Oh no."

The other ladies quickly said their good-byes, leaving Darren and Candy to themselves. She drew near and wrapped her arms around his neck. "I'm sure she's going to be fine. This isn't major, right?"

"I don't know. And even if it is, I doubt she'll crack the veneer to let us in to help. She's pretty self-sufficient."

"Oh, you might be surprised." A look of compassion came over Candy as she spoke. "I don't know if I've ever told you this, but my mom had cancer several years ago. Now, she's always been a real softie—a lot different from the way you've described your mom—but the illness really changed her. For the better, I mean. Yes, she went through a lot physically, but she came out of it a lot stronger, and more dependent on God. So, that's how I'm going to pray for your mom. That the Lord will use this situation to draw her to Him."

Darren nodded. "Thank you. I needed to hear that."

"He can do it. And your mom's in the perfect place to hear right now. He's got her full, undivided attention."

"True." Darren shook his head. "I feel so. . .conflicted. She's my mom, you know?"

"Of course."

"I love her, but she doesn't always make it easy. And now I'm scared something will happen to her before I've had a chance to really work on restoring our relationship. Not that I haven't tried in the past. I have. . ."

"Well, just think about what I've said. This illness is likely going to change her. She's facing her own mortality. And I'd be willing to bet God will use it as a catalyst to mend not just her relationship with you, but her relationship with your dad, as well."

"I hope you're right."

"Time will tell." She gave him a light peck on the cheek. "So, do you want to pray about it?"

He knew what she meant, of course. Right here. Right now.

"Sure. You already prayed inside. No reason to think we can't do the same out here." Darren took Candy's hands in his and began to pray. Then, after a time, she took over, praying for his mother's healing. . .both physical and emotional.

As Candy prayed, Darren realized just how different his relationship with Candy was from his parents' relationship.

*Lord, thank You for sending her to me. I'm going to seal the deal, Lord, just as soon as You give me the go-ahead. Gonna wrap up this Candy and take her home. . .for good.*

# eighteen

The day of the banquet arrived at last. Candy worked with the other women to prepare the ballroom at the Dorothy House. She brought in easels and large photos of Amelia Earhart, along with several other women who'd made such a huge difference in the industry over the years.

Once everything was in place, Candy, Anna, Brooke, and Shawneda stared at the room in silence.

"I'm so proud of you." Anna gave her hand a squeeze. "You're doing a great thing here."

"You think?" When they all nodded, she said, "I'm so excited. And I'm so grateful. None of this would have been possible without you. Have I told you how much I appreciate all of you?"

"Only twenty or thirty times," Brooke said with a crooked smile.

They all laughed and shared a group hug. Candy enjoyed the moment. It felt so good to have the support of her friends. And how good of Brooke to give so much of her time, especially in light of her wedding plans.

By six o'clock, both of the guest speakers had arrived, along with their spouses. Candy showed them to their seats and gave them the program schedule. She paused for a few minutes to talk to Margaret Franklin, the older of their two speakers. She paused a moment as she took in the woman's beautiful face. The wrinkles around her eyes were clearly laugh lines, judging from her joyous expression.

"I just want you to know how much it means to me that you've come." Candy couldn't hide her smile. "We're just so blessed to have you here."

"I'm the one who's blessed." Margaret gave her a motherly look. "I've asked the Lord to open any doors I'm to walk through, and He opened this one. I'm here because He's led me here. And I hope the stories I share will bring hope to all of you younger women. That's my plan, anyway."

"Oh, I'm sure it will."

Less than an hour later, the room filled with beautifully dressed people. Most were women, naturally, but a few had brought their spouses or boyfriends along. Lilly came with a handsome fellow she'd met at the library. . .an elementary school teacher. She buzzed with excitement as she introduced him to the group.

"Everyone, this is Phil. Phil, this is everyone."

They welcomed him in style, then Candy turned to Darren and whispered, "Will you hang out with him while we're working? Make him feel welcome?" Darren readily agreed.

Candy barely had time to blink before she was whisked away to deal with a technical issue. The PowerPoint presentation she'd prepared had a glitch. No problem. She'd get it straightened out.

At ten minutes till seven, her family arrived. She could hardly believe it when she saw a very pregnant Taffie heading in her direction. "No way. You're huge!"

"Well, thanks a lot." Taffie laughed, then pretended to pout.

"Oh, you know what I mean. You look radiant. You're glowing."

"Aw, thanks. I'm enjoying this part of the pregnancy. But that third trimester's sneaking up on me. . .and soon. Hope you plan to come home for the big event."

"I wouldn't miss it for the world." Candy gave her sister a hug, then turned her attention to her parents. "I'm so glad you came. This means the world to me. And if it weren't for the two of you. . ." She couldn't finish the sentence.

"Oh, don't make me cry." Her mother reached for a tissue and dabbed her eyes. "I'm already menopausal. And I'm about to be a grandmother. I cry at the drop of a hat now."

Something about that got Candy tickled. She laughed.

Until she looked at the clock. Five till seven. Better stay on top of things.

At seven ten, with everyone seated at their tables, Candy took the podium and welcomed their guests. She could hardly believe the crowd. And the room! It looked amazing. Her nerves almost got the better of her as she delivered her opening welcome. She fought her way past the tremor in her voice as she spoke.

"Good evening, everyone. I'm thrilled to welcome you to this, the first annual Newark Liberty International Airport banquet for women in aviation. We're about to be served our meal, but before we do, I'd like to specifically thank those who've worked so hard to make this evening possible." She began to reel off the names of the many people who'd come to her aid over the past few weeks, then paused to pray for the meal. Afterward, she told the crowd to hang onto its hats, that an awesome presentation would follow dinner.

But first things first. She'd made arrangements with the caterer to have a fabulous meal—prime rib, au gratin potatoes, and a vegetable medley, along with bread and yummy slices of cheesecake for dessert.

Candy took her place at the head table alongside the speakers. Their conversation was so lively that she almost let the time get away from her. At 7:40, just as dessert was being served, she made her way to the podium once again. With great joy, she introduced their first speaker.

Margaret Franklin rose and came to the microphone. She wrapped Candy in a tight embrace and whispered, "You go, girl! I'm so proud of you for putting together this fabulous event," in her ear. Then, with the assurance of a skilled public speaker, she stood before the crowd and told the story of her adventures as a young pilot in the '60s, focusing on some rather harrowing flights during the Vietnam War. The room was still and silent. People hung on her every word.

"I want to give a word of encouragement to the young women in the room tonight," Margaret said. "Those of you who might be thinking you've got it hard. Life is full of challenges. The question is not whether you will face challenges. We all do. The question is. . .will you triumph over them?"

Candy caught a glimpse of Darren, who sat at a nearby table. He had certainly faced his share of challenges of late. He'd shared many phone calls with his father in recent days. She knew he was concerned about his mother's health.

Tonight, however, he seemed more like the old Darren, the one with the ever-present smile and twinkling blue eyes. He gave her a wink and mouthed, "I love you." She grinned, felt her cheeks warm, then turned her attention back to the podium.

A hearty round of applause followed Margaret's heartfelt speech.

Next came the part Candy had been waiting for. She'd prepared a fabulous PowerPoint presentation, focusing on the history of women in aviation. The first photos had been harder to come by. . .female pilots from the 1920s. A few rare photos of the women who'd started the Ninety-Nines. Then the slide show traveled the decades. Everyone laughed at some of the uniforms worn by the women, especially in the thirties and forties, but Candy also heard several positive vocal responses from the crowd as the show progressed.

Finally, the photos transitioned to modern women. Women like Brooke, Anna, Lilly, Shawneda, and herself. Women like Norah, their next speaker.

When the presentation ended, Candy proudly introduced the petite young pilot, who came to the podium, her face awash with joy.

"How do I follow that?" Norah laughed. "Margaret was flying planes before I was even born. And she's flown to places I can only dream of flying." After a chuckle from the crowd, Norah spent the next ten minutes telling her story. How her parents had listened to her dreams of flying from early childhood on. How they'd supported her and helped her fulfill her dream.

At this point, Candy turned her attention to her parents and her siblings, who sat with Darren. She could barely restrain the tears as Norah talked. If not for the loving support of her family, her dream would never have become a reality.

*Cotton Candy, you've got your head in the clouds again.*

She could almost hear her father's teasing words. They'd bothered her as a child, but no longer. Now she loved the fact that her dreams. . .her childish, grandiose dreams. . .had finally become a reality.

And, oh! What a reality.

&

As the evening wound down, Darren found himself distracted. While he enjoyed the presentation immensely, and while he felt overwhelmed with pride at the amazing job Candy had done, he had something else on his mind. Something else altogether.

After weeks of praying, he'd finally come to a conclusion, one he felt sure the Lord had confirmed. Two conclusions, actually. As soon as the crowd cleared, he needed to talk to Candy. If she responded well to the first matter of business, he would make his move toward securing the second.

He reached into his pocket for the umpteenth time to make sure the tiny box was still there. Then again, where else would it be? His heart raced in anticipation. *First things first, Darren. Tell her what you're planning before you pop the question. And wait for the perfect moment. No point in jumping the gun.*

He watched as the crowd began to clear. Several people approached Candy, telling her what a great job she'd done. He couldn't help but agree. After several rounds of good-byes,

Candy kicked off her shoes and proclaimed it was time to get to work.

"We've got a lot to load up," she said, looking around the room. "The model planes and all of the other decorations need to be boxed up. And anything you see that belongs to us."

She and the other women went to work, loading up her car with the planes Darren and Jason had worked so hard to build. Even from here, every move she made drew him in. Did she have any idea how beautiful she was, especially in that blue gown? Did she know it made her upswept hair look like something out of a magazine? Could she even fathom that the sound of her laughter caused his heart rate to jump and his head to swim?

Soon. She would know it all very soon.

"Here, let me help you with that." Darren woke himself up from his daydreaming and went to work, grabbing one of the heavier boxes she had filled.

Finally, once the car was loaded and the room completely cleared, Darren and Candy said their good-byes to her family, promising to come down to Atlantic City for the birth of Taffie's baby.

When they were the last two remaining, Darren finally found the perfect opportunity to talk to Candy. . .alone.

"Sit a minute." He gestured at the bench outside the banquet hall.

"I'm tired, Darren. Can't we just—"

"It won't take long. But there's something I need to tell you."

"But I'm so worn out. Can't it wait until—"

"I've had something on my mind for ages." He put his hand in his pocket once more. *Yep. Still there. I'll get to that in a moment. But something else to deal with first. . .*

"What is it?" She yawned, then leaned back against the bench, her eyes half-closed.

"Something about my career, actually."

"Oh?" Her eyes popped open at that. "What about it? Has

something else happened at Eastway that I need to know about?"

"No. This isn't about Eastway."

"It's not?"

He sat next to her on the bench. "No. And before I tell you any of this, I want you to know that I've prayed it through. I've got a real peace about this. It's going to rock my world. . .our world. . .a little, but I know it will be worth it in the end." *And once you're onboard with this plan, I have an even bigger one.*

"I think you'd better spit it out. I'm getting nervous."

"Okay." He stood and began to pace, ready to deliver the speech he'd rehearsed in his head all evening.

She gave him a pensive look. "Darren, you're scaring me."

"Don't be scared." He turned to face her. "Okay, this is it. All of my life, I've wanted to fly."

"Right." She shrugged, then stifled another yawn.

"And flying for Eastway has been great. Most of the time. But in my heart, I want something more. Something different."

"What? Are you serious?" She began to wind her hair around her index finger, something she only did when nervous. "Like what?"

"Candy, I want to start my own charter service." He spoke the words as fast as possible, just wanting to get them out. Candy's mouth rounded in an *Ooo* that reminded him of Fred, his goldfish. He plowed ahead, hoping to get the hardest part over first. "I know. It doesn't make a lot of sense. I have a great job. But every time I think about flying, I think about doing it in a plane that I own."

"You're buying a plane?"

"Well, not today. And probably not tomorrow, either. But I've had my eyes on a Cessna 208. And Jimmy's been talking to me about this King Air a friend of his is selling. It's in tip-top shape. And we could grow from there."

"Wait. We? Are you talking about. . .you and me?"

*Yikes.* "Well, yes. And no. I'm actually talking about Jimmy. He and I would do this together. Between us, we could get the financial backing. I know we could. And if we start out small, then add jets later on, we'll have a huge range of aircraft and pricing to meet the needs of individuals at all income levels. And who knows. . .maybe at that point, you could come and fly with us, too. I mean, if you want to."

"I. . .I don't know." She stared at him, clearly confused. "I've only been at Eastway a couple months and I love it. I'm not saying I wouldn't ever want to do that, but right now it just doesn't make sense. And I'm not sure that you're thinking clearly, Darren. What you're talking about. . .it's going to cost a fortune. And it's risky. You've got great job security at Eastway. Why would you give all of that up?"

"I'm not saying I'd give up anything." He felt his patience wearing thin. "And this is something I've really prayed about. Jimmy's been checking into the licenses we'll need. And he's been researching to see what the competition is charging for their services, so we'll know what to charge."

"Okay. . ." She leaned back against the bench, a look of exhaustion on her face.

"Candy, think about it. I could do away with a lot of the stresses related to flying for someone else. And best of all, I could be living my dream."

"Living your dream." She paused a moment, then sighed.

"You, of all people, know about dreams. So, I thought you'd. . ." He didn't finish. Suddenly he felt completely deflated.

"Darren, I want you to be happy." Her smiled seemed a bit forced. "I'm just. . .surprised. And I'm so tired that none of this is really registering right now. Would you mind if we talked about this tomorrow night, after I get back from my flight to Minneapolis? I'm sure it'll all make more sense then."

"I guess." He tried not to let his disappointment show. Still, he had to wonder how she could get so excited about women in aviation. . .and couldn't even muster up the tiniest bit of enthusiasm for his project.

Besides, if he didn't get past this first question, he'd never get to the second one. The one where he would pull the ring from his pocket and slip it on her finger.

Determined not to give much away with his expression, he walked with her to her car. All the while, he tried to formulate a new plan regarding the intended proposal.

As they walked, she grumbled about how much her feet ached after wearing heels all night. Then she transitioned into a lengthy dissertation about Margaret Hamilton's magnificent speech. Darren tried to get a word in edgewise, but couldn't.

*Lord, help me out here. Please. Everything is unraveling. I need some direction.*

Just as they reached the car, she paused for breath. *Perfect opportunity. I'm going to do this. . .right now. Even if the timing isn't what I thought it would be.*

In that very moment, his cell phone rang. Darren groaned and pushed the volume key to mute, not even looking at the number.

"Someone's calling pretty late. Must be important."

He glanced down at the number and his heartbeat skipped to double time. "It's my dad." He answered right away. "Dad?"

"Son?" His father's voice was barely recognizable. "Did I wake you?"

"No, it's fine. I'm still up. What's happened?"

"Your mother. . .well, she's had a heart attack. It's a bad one."

A lump rose in Darren's throat and he felt the sting of tears. "I–I'll be on the next flight out, Dad."

"Thank you. I really need you here. I'm so. . .I don't know what to do. She's always the one who handles things. . .like this."

"Tell me where you're at."

"UCSD. Fourth floor. ICU."

"I'm coming. I'll call when I have a plan of action. And Dad. . ."

"Yes?"

"Please tell Mom I love her." It felt like a rock lodged in Darren's throat as the words were spoken.

"I'll do that," his father whispered.

Darren ended the call, then turned to Candy, not even trying to stop the overflow of emotions. In one instant, everything had changed. The news about his business ideas would have to wait. The proposal would have to wait. Right now, there was someone in California he needed to see. . .and the sooner, the better.

# nineteen

Candy entered the apartment at a quarter till one, fighting the mixture of emotions that threatened to overtake her. After stopping by Darren's house to help him pack, she'd driven him to the airport, where he'd managed to catch a flight to San Diego with a brief layover in Phoenix. For now, all they could do was pray. And wait.

Her heart twisted in several different directions at once. In spite of the news about Darren's mom, she still longed to celebrate the evening's events. Together the women had pulled off a smashing night, after all. Everyone said so.

Just as quickly, realization set in. *Lord, You did it. We could never have put this together on our own, and we certainly couldn't have raised forty thousand dollars in scholarships for women who want to fly.* She still marveled at the fact that so many people had been willing to make donations above and beyond the cost of their ticket to the event. And a couple of corporations had come onboard, as well, promising support both now and in the future. This news thrilled her.

She opened the door to her bedroom to find that Lilly was already fast asleep. Doing her best to remain quiet, Candy tiptoed to her dresser and opened a drawer to pull out her PJs.

As she dressed for bed, Candy replayed the night in her mind. Over and over again she thought about Margaret Franklin and the words she'd spoken from the podium. Her stories had held everyone captivated. What a difference one woman had made in the industry.

*Lord, I want to be like that. I want You to use me.*

After brushing her teeth, she crawled under the covers

and rested her head against the pillow. As weariness set in, everything from the banquet began to run together. The women. The stories. The decorations. The pretty dresses. The speeches.

Darren.

He'd been there all evening, right in the thick of things. And he'd obviously had a wonderful time, judging from his reactions during the event. Before the phone call from his dad, of course. But all that stuff about starting a charter service. . .was he really serious? Would he give up a steady job to set off on his own in a risky business? How in the world could he fund such a venture?

*Nah. He's just dreaming out loud.*

Maybe.

Who was she to question his dreams? Wasn't she the queen of dreams? *I should have offered more support.*

And now. . .the situation with his mother.

Candy's breath caught in her throat as she realized all that Darren was facing at once. And alone, no less. If only she could've gone with him. That would have changed everything. Maybe, through the haze of emotions, they could have made sense of things. She hadn't exactly been a bastion of support when he'd told her his ideas, had she? But exhaustion had set in. Surely he understood that.

*Exhaustion. Hmm.*

She glanced at the clock and groaned. One fifteen? Her flight to Minneapolis left at nine. If she could get her thoughts to stop fast-forwarding through her brain like a sepia tone movie, she might just get some sleep.

❧

Darren flew through the night, this time in a first-class seat. He spent much of the time in prayer for his mother. He wasn't sure about her walk with God. Maybe he'd have an opportunity to talk with her about that when he arrived. He hoped.

With nothing else to do—and with so much on his mind—Darren spent the two and a half hours between Newark and Phoenix interceding for the one person he'd always had the hardest time praying for.

*Lord, it feels like the rug's been pulled out from under me. I've lost my bearings. Everything is in turmoil. My job. My mom's health. My relationship with Candy.* He swallowed hard at that one. One thing he hadn't counted on was the lack of enthusiasm from Candy at his news about the business venture.

*Lord, show me what to do. I need Your guidance. Show me what to say to my mom and what not to say. And help me figure out where to go from here. . .with my career. With my personal life. With my future.*

He leaned back against the seat and plugged in the earphones to his MP3 player. A worship song played in the background. He listened to the words, finally able to calm down. They reminded him that God was bigger than any problems he might face. . .now or in the future. Now, if he could only go on believing that after the song ended.

Darren finally managed to doze off. He knew he'd need his sleep. Likely he wouldn't get much once he arrived in San Diego.

When he reached Phoenix for the layover, Darren called his father. "Any change?"

"No. She's. . ." His father choked back tears. "She's pretty heavily medicated right now, Darren. And I don't know what to expect. They're not really telling me much, and I don't want to speculate."

"I'll be there in an hour and a half, Dad. You sound exhausted."

"I am."

"Well, try to get some sleep. And when I get there, we can take turns watching over her."

"Okay. I'm glad you're coming." After a moment's hesitation, his father added, "Want me to pick you up at the airport?"

"No. I'll catch a cab. You just stay with Mom."

They ended the call, and Darren prepared to board his next flight. For once, he wanted to be free from airplanes. . .to have his feet on solid ground. On the other hand, as the nose of the plane tipped upward. . .as they took to the skies, he was reminded once again of the Lord's earlier admonition to soar above his circumstances.

Only one way to do that.

He'd have to completely let go of the controls and leave the piloting to God.

֍

Candy awoke a couple of times in the night. Each time she prayed for Darren and his mom. She couldn't shake the nagging feeling that something was wrong. Very wrong.

On the other hand, she knew better than to let fear get the better of her. So, every time fear rose up, she prayed all the harder.

*Lord, I don't know what's going on here, but You do. I just ask that You take control, Father. Take my emotions and my fears. And be with Darren as he travels.*

Darren.

Her heart grew heavy at the mention of his name. How would she manage these next few days without him? Determined to sleep, she rolled over and gave the pillow a firm whack.

She must've made more noise than she knew because Lilly sat up in her bed and began to stammer. "W—what happened?"

"Nothing. Sorry. Go back to sleep."

"Okay." Lilly lay back down and mumbled, "You, too, Candy. We've got a long day ahead of us tomorrow."

"Yes, I know."

After a few minutes, Candy's eyes grew heavy, and she found herself drifting off. . .at last.

# twenty

On Sunday morning Candy awoke just in time to catch a quick shower and head to the airport. Thankfully, Lilly would be on the same flight, so they shared a ride.

Though Lilly chattered at will as she drove, Candy couldn't stop thinking about Darren. And though she'd tried a couple of times to call him, he wasn't picking up. Likely he'd turned his cell phone off in the hospital. Still, she didn't feel right about taking off without talking to him. They hadn't ended things on the best of notes last night.

And there was something else, too. Just before the call from his father, he'd looked as if he wanted to say something to her. He'd pulled back at the last minute with a sad look on his face. But, why?

*I deflated his ego. I didn't support him when he told me about his dream. I'm a sorry excuse for a girlfriend.*

Before boarding the 747 to Minneapolis, she made one last attempt to call him. Again, he didn't pick up. She shut off her phone and headed to the plane, ready to put this day behind her. As always, she prayed as she settled into the cockpit. And, in spite of the ups and downs of the last twenty-four hours, felt comfortable behind the wheel.

Adam Landers, her captain, looked at her with a smile. "Minneapolis, here we come."

"Yep." She gave him a confident smile. "Then it's back home to Newark. All in a day's work."

"All in a day's work," he repeated.

She offered him a smile. . .and then they took to flight.

❧

Darren paced the halls of the hospital, talking to his father.

143

His mother's condition appeared to be stabilizing. And a recent visit with the cardiologist confirmed that her medically induced coma would soon be behind them.

"I want you to be prepared for a long haul," the doctor admonished. "She's got quite a journey ahead of her. It's going to take patience and a firm hand. Her best chance will be a serious change in diet and a low-stress environment."

Darren had cringed at that last part. He couldn't imagine the words *low stress* used in the same sentence as his mother. And how would his dad cope? She'd be a tough case, no doubt. Did his father have it in him to make her line up and walk straight? Only time would tell.

He made his way back into his mother's room, standing at her bedside in quiet reflection. Sometime later, the craziness of the past several hours caught up with him and his eyes grew heavy. Darren took a seat in the chair to his mother's right. His father—who looked equally as exhausted—sat opposite him on the left side of the bed.

Just after noon California time, Darren received a call from Jason. It jarred him from his slumber. He answered right away.

"Hey, thanks for calling." He lowered his voice, so as not to wake his father, who slept in a nearby chair. "I guess you heard about my mom."

"Yes." Jason's voice trembled as he spoke. "And I'm praying. But, Darren. . .are you watching the news?"

"The news?" He glanced up at the television, which hadn't been turned on all day. "No. Should I be? What's happening?"

"There's a. . .well, you'd just better look and see. I'm watching CNN, but I'm sure this is on every major news station."

Darren reached for the remote and clicked on the television. Immediately his heart went to his throat as he saw the news flash. EASTWAY PILOT ATTEMPTS EMERGENCY LANDING IN NEWARK.

"Darren, what's happening?" His father came awake with a start.

"It's. . ." He couldn't finish the sentence. Darren watched, gripped with fear, as the 747 pointed itself at the runway, nose gear still up.

The news reporter's voice jarred him. "The control tower has confirmed that the front landing gear of Eastway flight 4582 is not down. But it looks like the pilot is trying to bring the plane down without the landing gear. He's got the aircraft under control for the moment but. . .ah, I've just been told the first officer—a female—is actually flying the plane while the captain works to rectify the problem. She's doing an admirable job of—"

*Oh, Lord. . .no. Please, no.*

The reporter's voice paused for a few seconds. Just when the plane looked as if it would come in for an attempted landing, the nose lifted once again and it disappeared from view.

"Not sure what just happened there," the reporter picked back up again. "Must've had a change of heart." The camera zoomed in on the plane as it continued to ascend. "This has got to be frightening for the passengers and the crew. And for the family members watching."

"Darren?" Jason's voice came over the phone line, startling him back to attention. "Are you there?"

"I'm here. Jason, that's. . ."

"I know. And I'm praying. I'm going to hang up now so we can focus on doing that."

"No, wait. The Bible says if two or more agree in prayer. . ." Darren didn't take time to finish the scripture. Instead, he began to pray aloud from the depths of his soul. . .for Candy and the other crew members on the 747 and for the passengers and people on the ground as well.

Just as he finished, the reporter came back on. "It looks as if that's foam they're applying to the runway, to reduce the risk of fire when the plane makes its final attempt."

"Could you not say *final* in that tone?" Darren directed his words to the television.

"We've just confirmed there are seventy-three passengers onboard the Eastway flight, including one infant and one wheelchair-bound passenger." The reporter went off on a tangent about the various passengers, but Darren barely heard a word. Everything seemed to be moving in slow motion, including the reporter's voice.

"Darren, God is in control." Jason's voice again. Calm. Controlled. "We can trust Him."

"Yes. I know."

"Darren, do you know someone on that plane?" His father's concerned voice brought him back to reality.

"I do."

The camera flashed to the aircraft, which had made a wide circle and now pointed itself at the runway once again.

"C'mon, Candy. You can do this."

"Candy?" His father whispered the word. "Your Candy?"

He nodded.

"It looks as if the pilot is going to make another attempt." The reporter's voice rose with anticipation as the plane began to descend.

Darren began to pray, silently at first, and then aloud as he watched. "You can do it, Candy," he whispered, when he'd finished praying. "You've been trained. You know what to do. Just listen to your gut. Do what you've been taught."

"You can do it, girl," his father joined in.

Then, as if she'd planned for this moment her entire life, Candy brought the aircraft down to the ground. It skidded off to the left of the runway, wreaking havoc with the foam. Darren wanted to scream. To jump for joy. Instead, he looked at his father with tears in his eyes, overcome with relief.

The reporter's voice kicked in. "Folks, she's done it. That's some first officer. She pulled off a textbook landing."

Darren's hands began to tremble. He heard Jason's voice on the other end of the phone. "Thank You, Jesus," and added a tearful, "Amen."

He watched in awe as the aircraft came to a complete stop. After a moment's pause, the reporter jumped back in with his comments. "Looks like they'll be implementing an emergency evacuation."

"Wow. I've only seen this in the movies." Darren's father stood close to the television, watching in rapt awe.

"Yes, they've just deployed the chutes," the reporter continued. He went on to describe in detail the layout of a 747, honing in on where the emergency exits were located.

"I don't believe this." Darren shook his head. His father was right. It really was like watching a movie. . .only, the woman he loved was playing the lead role.

The reporter's inflection changed. "Folks, we've just been joined by Marcus Blackwell, a spokesman with the Newark Airport Authority. Mr. Blackwell, what can you tell us about what we've just seen? And when will we know the condition of the passengers and crew?"

Another voice, this one a bit calmer, took over. "The pilot of Eastway flight 4582 reported the faulty landing gear at 2:52 p.m. Newark time."

"And when something like this happens, the pilot has been trained to respond accordingly?" the reporter asked.

"Every pilot is taught to prepare for the worst, and is trained accordingly. The pilots aboard the Eastway flight today worked with the tower to bring the aircraft down in the safest possible manner."

Darren continued to watch as people began to descend the emergency ramps. He'd had nightmares about flights like this. Likely every pilot had.

"As you can see, we've got fire and rescue personnel on the ground to receive any people who might need to be evaluated or transported to hospitals," Mr. Blackwell continued. "At this time we have no word as to the condition of the passengers or crew, but we are very relieved, as you might imagine."

Relieved? Relieved hardly described the feeling that swept

over Darren as he watched the passengers exit the plane. *Why am I in California instead of Newark? I need to be there for her. I've got to leave. Got to—*

His heart nearly leaped into his throat as a weak voice interrupted the moment. "D–darren? Darren, is that you?"

He turned toward the bed to face his mother, whose eyes were half-opened.

"I'm here, Mama." He rushed to her side and gripped her hand. "You rest easy now. Rest easy. Everything's going to be all right."

"Thank you for coming," she whispered, then squeezed his hand. "We need you right now."

"I–I'm here."

Yes, he was here. Oh, but how he wished he could be in two places at once.

◈

Candy sat in the cockpit, shaking like a leaf. For a moment she felt dizzy, then a wave of nausea swept over her. "I'm going to be sick." The captain reached for a bag and pressed it into her hand. Candy sat, breathing deeply, until the feeling passed. Even so, she still felt woozy.

Adam—the captain who'd kept his cool throughout the ordeal—reached out to touch her arm. "Candy, I have something to say. You did an amazing job. Thanks to you, our passengers and crew are safely home."

"No, not thanks to me." She shook her head, unable to take the credit. "I had nothing to do with it, trust me. Only the Lord could have accomplished that."

"Well, He apparently used you to help." Adam nodded. "And I couldn't have taken on the job of troubleshooter without you actually flying the plane. But just prepare yourself. I'd say there's going to be an outpouring from the community. And you're about to get swarmed by the media. Are you up for it?"

"The media?"

*Man. After weeks of trying to stay out of the limelight at*

*Eastway, suddenly I'm thrust into the spotlight in front of the entire nation?*

"That landing was textbook. I can't imagine doing a better job myself. And I don't think you'd be giving yourself too much credit if you admitted you did a fine job."

"T—thank you."

Adam rose to his feet and looked her way. "Ready to get off of this bird?"

"Mm-hmm." She nodded. "Am I ever."

"Well, just be prepared. I have a feeling we're about to be inundated."

One look outside convinced her he was right. With so many ambulances and fire trucks about, they were sure to be swamped with people. And where there was a story, there were sure to be journalists.

A shiver went down her spine as she thought about that. *Journalists. News.* Man. Talk about throwing a kink in her plans to keep a low profile.

She and Adam reached the door where the emergency chutes were in place. With all of their passengers safely on the ground, they could take their final ride toward freedom.

Funny. All she could think of as she slid down the chute was what she'd told Darren that day on the Cessna 400. "I've never jumped out of a plane before."

And though this probably wasn't the kind of jump he had in mind, she had to admit. . .it looked like there was a first time for everything.

When she reached the ground, people swarmed her. Medics, police. . .she could scarcely breathe for all of the people. And they all talked on top of one another. "Are you hurt?"

"Great job!"

"You should win an Emmy for that performance."

"We're so proud of you."

She and Adam were taken by patrol car to the Eastway

offices, where she was met with the craziest mob of media folks she'd ever seen.

*I didn't even know we had this many newspapers and television stations in Newark.*

Turned out folks from the New York media had already arrived and were ready for a story. A national story.

More than an hour of craziness slipped by before she was finally able to reach for her cell phone to call Darren. She stared transfixed at the phone, noticing for the first time how many times he'd called her. She'd missed every one, thanks to the chaos.

"Better put his mind at ease."

She punched in his number, tears welling. Only one thing could make her feel better. Scratch that. Only one *person* could make her feel better. And he was on the other side of the country, handling a crisis of his own.

## twenty-one

Darren paced the halls of the hospital, nearly frantic. He finally managed to reach Brooke. "Have you heard from her?"

"She's up at the Eastway offices, Darren. They've got her secluded. I'm sure she's going to call you."

"Who was on that flight with her?"

"Adam Landers. And Lilly."

"Lilly. Really?" His heart twisted. "And Adam." Both friends. And both very much alive, thanks to the Lord's intervention and Candy's skillful landing.

"I'm still trying to reach Candy, but if you hear from her—"

"I'll have her call you, I promise." After a moment's pause, Brooke asked, "How's your mom, Darren?"

"Awake. Ornery. The doctors are going to perform some sort of procedure on her in a couple of days to see about clearing up the blockage. And then she's going to have a major change in lifestyle. Just pray she'll go along with it, and pray for my dad, too, okay? He's going to have to step up to the plate and. . . well, he's got his work cut out for him."

"Of course. Would you like me to pray right now?"

A wave of peace washed over him. Darren slumped in a chair. "W–would you? I feel like the biggest wimp on planet Earth. It'll be good to have someone agree with me in prayer."

"Of course. And hey, I head up the prayer chain for the singles group, so I'm used to praying over the phone." She began to pray, starting with a joyous praise for God's hand of protection, which He'd placed on both Darren's mother and on Candy and the crew aboard flight 4582. Then she shifted gears, praying for healing for his mom and provision for his father. By the time she ended, Darren had tears in his eyes.

"Thanks, Brooke."

"You're welcome."

She'd no sooner said the words than a *beep* interrupted their call. He looked at the number and practically dropped the phone. "Gotta go. It's Candy."

Without so much as a good-bye, he clicked over, speaking her name undergirded by emotion.

"Darren?" Her trembling voice showed her feelings immediately.

"Candy, I'm here," he managed. "I'm so glad to hear your voice. I've been worried sick."

"I knew you would be. I wanted to call right away, but they wouldn't let me. You should have seen it. There were so many people, and they had so many questions. I felt like I was on trial."

"I'll bet. But you're okay?"

"Physically. My insides are mush. And I don't know if I'll ever be able to get back in the cockpit again. I. . ." She began to cry.

"You will. I know you. You're great at this, Candy. And you're called to it. You can't give up. You've got to get right back in there and get to work."

"Well, not today. I think I'm going to go home and take a hot bath. Maybe eat some Chinese food. Then I'm going to pull the covers up over my head and pretend none of this ever happened."

"I'd probably do exactly the same thing. Only I'd eat a cheeseburger, not Chinese."

She offered up a nervous laugh, then added, "I wish you were here."

"Me, too." He paused, and tried not to let his emotions get the better of him. She needed him to be strong. "Do you want to talk about what happened, or wait till after you've had some food?"

"I can talk about it, I guess. But first tell me about your

mom. I've been so concerned about her. And when I saw that you'd called so many times, I was afraid. . ."

"She's better." Darren quickly filled her in on his mother's condition, honing in on the part of the story where his mother had asked him to pray.

"She was barely awake, but she knew who I was. And she had tears in her eyes. I think God is working on her, Candy. Just like you predicted."

"She's a captive audience. Kind of like I was in that cockpit today."

"So, you want to talk about it?"

"Yeah." She paused a moment, then began to tell her story, her voice shaking every step of the way. "We'd had the smoothest flight ever. Nothing suspicious. And I had no reason to think the landing gear would stick. Our landing in Minneapolis was great. No indications of any problems." She paused a moment. "A lot of things went through my mind in that cockpit once I realized we were in trouble. Of course, I thought about all the things I would miss if I. . ."

"Don't even say it." A shiver ran down his spine just thinking of the what-ifs.

"Well, I know where I'm going when the time comes," she reminded him, "so it wasn't really a fear about that part. It was more about the responsibility I had to protect the passengers. And Lilly. And Adam. The responsibility was overwhelming, really."

"I have to admit, my faith just flew right out the window when I got the call." He pursed his lips. "And I went into a panic when I watched the news footage. I told Brooke, I'm a spiritual wimp in a crisis. I never knew that till now."

"No you're not." The tenderness in her voice brought him comfort.

"Well, just the thought of losing you. . ." His eyes filled with tears. "I couldn't stand it."

"That's what I was about to say. I am ready to go, if the

Lord calls me home. I'm confident of that because I've put my trust in Jesus. But on the other hand, the idea of all the things you and I would miss. . ." She paused. "I don't want to miss a day with you."

"Me, either."

"And I want you to be happy, Darren."

"Happy?" He could hardly stand the joy that flooded over him. "I am happy. You make me the happiest man on earth."

"I'm talking about something other than our relationship. You're content working for Eastway, but I don't think you're really happy. It doesn't put a sparkle in your eye."

"Ah."

"You tried to tell me last night, and I was too tired to listen. Or maybe I didn't want to listen because I don't handle change well. But God really dealt with me in the night. Reminded me of what a dreamer I've always been. It only makes sense that I'd fall in love with a dreamer, too."

"Ah." He smiled. "I've got my head in the clouds. Is that what you're trying to say?"

"Something like that." She laughed, but grew serious very quickly afterward. "Remember that day on the Cessna 400? You flew me over the English countryside. And a castle. And Big Ben."

"Right."

"You were free to dream that day. To see the impossibilities as possibilities. That's one of the things I love most about flying. It's something that, when we're children, seems impossible. And yet, we're doing it. We're spreading our wings and flying. So, go ahead and dream. I'll dream right alongside you. You tried to share your heart last night. . .to talk about your plans for the future, but I was too tired to listen. And it haunted me today in that cockpit. I should have taken the time to really hear everything you wanted to say."

"Wait. Are you saying you're okay with the idea of the charter service?"

"I'm okay with it."

"Candy, I've really been praying about this."

"I know. Me, too. Well, today mostly. But you know what? I totally think you should do it."

"You do? What changed your mind?"

"Well, my near-death experience, for one thing."

He grimaced.

"I had a thousand things flash through my mind when I was circling the airport that second time. And, strange as it may sound, one of those things was your charter plane service." She laughed. "I was thinking, actually, how much easier it would be to attempt a landing with a smaller plane with the landing gear up."

"Hope I never have to find out personally."

"I hope you don't, either. It was scary." She paused a moment. "But when I thought about you running your own company, one thing stood out. You're so good with people. You are funny and sweet and—"

"Wait." He grinned. "Not that I don't appreciate the endorsement. Flattery will get you everywhere, after all. But what does this have to do with flying small planes?"

"Oh, everything." Her words were filled with encouragement. "When you're flying for Eastway, you really don't have much opportunity to connect with the passengers. Your whole job— well, except for the part where you greet them as they come onboard or when they're leaving—is in that cockpit."

"Right."

"Well, that works well for me. I'm fine with that. But you"—her voice grew more animated—"you've got an evangelist's heart. I can see you really interacting with your passengers if you have your own service."

"Yes. Me, too." He nodded. "And these days so many executives in the corporate world are chartering private planes. I really think this could be a profitable business. And you're right. . .it's a great way to get to know people. Establish relationships, not just with individuals, but with the kinds of people who hire private planes. . .political people who need the added security, and even sports teams." His excitement grew as he continued. "And I really meant what I said the other night. I'll start with a couple of smaller planes, and maybe—say in a year or so—add a Boeing Business Jet. Or two."

"Or three." She giggled. "Sounds like you're talking about adding children to our brood."

Both of them stopped talking at once. Darren grinned as he pondered her words. They gave him such hope.

Candy finally interrupted the awkward silence. "I, um, I have no idea why I just said that. I wasn't implying—"

He laughed, mostly out of relief. "Well, I do. I plan to add children to our brood." He grinned. "Not that we'll use the word *brood* on a regular basis, but you know what I mean."

"So. . ."

"You know me. I'm the funny guy. But you've just opened the door for me to ask this question that's been burning a hole in my heart and my pocket for the past twenty-four hours."

"W–what?"

"This is the goofiest way in the world to do this, but I. . . I'm asking you to be my—"

"Wait. A–are you proposing. . .over the phone?"

"I know, I know." He shook his head, thinking about how ridiculous this was. "It's dumb. I want to hold you and tell you how much I love you. I want to show you the ring that I had in my pocket last night, the first time I planned to ask this question."

"Y–you had a ring?" She groaned. "Oh, man. I totally blew it, didn't I?"

"Well, I think we both did. I picked the wrong time to start the conversation. You were exhausted and. . ." He paused, thinking things through. "Actually you've had a pretty rough day today, too, so my timing is probably even worse now."

"Oh no it's not. Keep going, you. You're not stopping now."

He stood up and began to pace. "I've thought about this a hundred times. Jason tried to help me come up with something funny to say to pop the question."

"Like?" Her voice now had that dreamy childlike quality he'd grown to love.

He tried to match it with his enthusiasm. "Well, like 'Come fly with me' or 'Love is in the air.' I told him he was crazy. And I stopped cold every time I rehearsed the line, 'I'd like you to be Mrs. Candy Furst.'"

She laughed. "Oh, no! I can't believe I never thought about that before. Candy Furst. What a name."

"Trust me, I thought about it. In fact, I wondered if it would be enough to keep you from saying yes."

"Oh, I'm saying yes, all right."

His heart kicked into overdrive. "R–really? Even without a ring?"

"Oh, I'm holding you to the ring. But I think I can wait till you get back to let you slip it on my finger."

"I'm going to find the most romantic way to do that, I promise." Ideas began to click. "What do you think? A walk in the park? Maybe somewhere along the boardwalk? The beach at sunset?"

"Darren?"

"Yes?"

"The bride-to-be isn't supposed to plan her own proposal."

"Right, right." He sat down once again. "I know. I'm just so excited. I don't want to blow this again."

"Um, I've already said yes. How could you blow it?"

*She actually said yes!*

Candy began to giggle. "So, I go from being Cotton Candy to Candy Furst. Trading up, I guess."

"I hope you really feel that way."

"Oh, yeah. I'm trading up all right."

A thousand thoughts rolled around in Darren's head. There was so much to do. He had to get home. . .and soon. Funny, the minute he thought about home, another thought occurred to him. "One more thing."

"What's that?"

"When I get back to Newark, I'm buying Fred a girlfriend."

"Excuse me?" She laughed. "Say that again."

"Fred. My goldfish. He's been swimming around in that tank of his completely alone for far too long. He needs a wife. And a brood of baby goldfish."

"You mean a school, don't you?"

"Whatever."

Candy laughed. "We'll go to the pet store and pick out the perfect bride for Fred. But in the meantime, you take care of your mama. And give her my love. Tell her she's got to get well. We need her to come to a wedding."

"Will do. And Candy. . .I love you."

❧

"I love you, too." As Candy spoke the words, a rush of emotion overtook her. Everything she'd been through—last night's banquet, today's near-disaster, Darren's mother, the proposal—all hit her at once. She began to cry. No, not cry. Sob. Deep, gut-wrenching sobs.

Darren responded immediately. "Are you okay?"

"Y–yes." She spoke through the tears. "This has just been such an amazing, crazy, wonderful, terrible day." She paused to dab her eyes, then took a couple of deep breaths to get things under control. "We're going to have quite a story to tell our brood of children someday."

"Which story?" he asked. "The one where I messed up the proposal or the one where you made the national news?"

"Both." She laughed. "We're a fine pair, aren't we?"

"We are." He grew silent for a moment. "But seriously, we are a fine pair, Candy. You're strong in the areas where I'm weak. My perfect helpmate."

"And vice versa," she whispered.

"And I love you more than. . .than flying. More than

dreaming. More than anything. . .except the One who brought us together."

"Me, too."

After a couple more "I love you's," Candy ended the call, her mind reeling.

Darren had been carrying a ring in his pocket last night at the banquet? He'd planned to propose on the steps of the Dorothy House. And she'd botched it! Botched it! But God, in His own humorous way, had redeemed the moment.

*Who else ever received a proposal by phone?*

Not that she minded. Not one little bit.

But never mind all that! Candy had phone calls to make. Likely her parents were still worried sick about the news story. She'd fill them in. Tell them the story of how, in one lone day, she'd nearly lost her life. . .then gained it all over again.

## twenty-two

Exactly one year to the day after Candy's fated flight, she prepared to don her wedding dress for a trip down the aisle.

Well, not exactly an aisle. Getting married in the middle of a runway at Essex County Airport made the whole aisle thing a bit problematic. Still, with the white rental chairs set up a la church-style, they'd concocted something that looked and felt like a center aisle.

Not that anyone expected anything traditional or normal from Candy and Darren. Hardly. These days folks had figured out that the happy couple could be a little on the flighty side. And flighty they would remain.

Now, as she stood in Darren's office at the airport with her bridesmaids soon to arrive, a thousand things went through her mind. *Did I bring everything I needed from home? When are my sisters going to get here? Where in the world is Darren taking me on our honeymoon? Why is he being so secretive?*

A rap on the door caught her attention. Her mother popped her head inside. "We're here!"

"Mama!" She ushered her mother into the room and started talking a mile a minute.

"Wait." Her mother backed up with a stunned expression. "Why are you still dressed in jeans? Shouldn't you be getting ready?"

"I need help with my dress so I was waiting on the girls. Brooke was here a while ago, but had to, um. . ."

"What?"

"Take a potty break. She's six months pregnant, you know."

"Ah. That's right. I'd forgotten about their little surprise package."

160

Candy smiled, remembering the day she'd gotten the news. Brooke and Jason had only been married three months at the time, and they'd hardly planned for a baby. But God had other ideas.

"Hey, speaking of babies. . ." Candy gave her mother an imploring look. "Where are—"

"Taffie's here with Maddy. She's in the bathroom, changing her diaper. You'll see them in a minute."

Another rap on the door caught their attention. Her father stuck his head in. "Wow. Great dress."

"Very funny, Pop." She laughed and pointed to the dress, which hung on a hook above the door. "This is it. Your hard-earned dollars at work."

"Very pretty." He entered the room, closing the door behind him. "So, we bought this one with taffy money. Oh, speaking of taffy."

"Yes?"

"We brought a couple of big bags of our latest best seller—wedding cake flavor. Thought it would be a nice addition."

"Of course."

Her father settled into the chair behind the desk. "So, where are you two going on your honeymoon?"

"I have no idea." She turned toward the mirror to continue putting on makeup.

"Seriously? I thought Darren was just messing with me when he wouldn't tell me."

She looked up with mascara wand in hand. "He won't tell me either. But he instructed me to pack for moderate weather, whatever that means."

"So, no place tropical."

"Guess not." She turned back to the mirror. "I do know we're taking the 208 to La Guardia and flying out commercial from there. But he won't tell me our destination."

"That's kind of what it's like walking with God, too." Her mother smiled. "You can only see so far out over the horizon.

But you really don't know what's beyond that." She paused and smiled. "I think it's better that way. Makes the journey ahead more of an adventure."

"True." Candy's eyes filled with tears, thinking of all the Lord had already done in her life. Could she possibly handle more of His goodness?

Their conversation was interrupted by the sound of a baby's cry. Taffie entered holding baby Maddy, now eight months old. Candy *ooh*ed and *aah*ed over her gorgeous niece. "Taffie, she's prettier than ever. And look at this dress! It's darling."

"Yes, she's a little doll, isn't she? Looks just like Ryan."

"No, she looks like her mama." Candy ran her fingertip along baby Maddy's soft cheek. "She's a Carini, for sure."

"That she is." Pop grinned. "Not that either of you girls are Carinis anymore. Taffie's an Antonelli. And now you're about to. . ." He grinned, not saying it.

"Pop, don't."

"Well, I just have one question. Now that you're the 'Furst lady,' does that mean you get to live in the White House?" He slapped his knee. "C'mon, that was a good one, you have to admit."

"Funny. But with all the politicians Darren is flying back and forth, you never know. The possibilities are endless."

Another rap sounded at the door and Tangie stuck her head inside. "Howdy, y'all. Just moseyed into town from my rehearsal."

"Oh?" Candy looked her way with a smile.

"It's a melodrama," Tangie explained. "I got the role of sweet Nell. Snidley Whiplash is going to tie me to the tracks, but Dudley Do-Right will rescue me just in the nick of time."

"Ah. Now here's a girl who's destined to carry the Carini name for a while longer," Pop said, rising to meet her.

"Thanks a lot." She rolled her eyes as she stepped into the room.

"Tangie." Candy gasped as she got a close look at her younger sister. She could hardly believe it. Tangie had dyed her hair back to its original brown. And the gorgeous blue bridesmaid dress covered up her tattoos. She looked downright beautiful. "You look. . . gorgeous."

Tangie's cheeks turned pink. "Aw, stop. You're embarrassing me."

"Like that would be possible." Candy laughed. She glanced at the clock on the wall, then turned to her father. "Um, Pop? It's a quarter to two. Taffie and I really need to get dressed."

"I can take a hint."

"Will you take the baby to Ryan?" Taffie asked. "His mom is going to watch her during the ceremony."

"Well, of course."

Candy watched as her father took his granddaughter in his arms and then backed out of the room, leaving the women to their own devices.

Brooke joined them moments later and the girls went to work, first getting Taffie ready, then getting Candy into her gown. Her mother zipped it up, then they all stood back and stared.

"Wow," Brooke said. "You look amazing."

"Doesn't she?" Candy's mother agreed. Then the tears started. "I'm sorry. I didn't mean to get to emotional. It's just. . . my girls are growing up. And all these weddings. . ."

"This is certainly going to be one no one will forget," Brooke added.

"You know, I thought my wedding was different." Taffie drew near and the two sisters stood side by side, looking at their reflections in the full-length mirror that leaned against the wall. "Getting married on the beach was pretty amazing. But I have to admit, getting married in the middle of a runway. . .that's pretty adventurous."

"You know what a dreamer I've always been," Candy said. "I love an adventure."

"Me, too." Taffie slipped an arm around her waist and gave her a squeeze.

Tangie stood apart from the others, quieter than usual. When she turned around, Candy saw the shimmer of tears in her younger sister's eyes.

"What's wrong?" She walked over to her and grabbed her hand.

"Oh, nothing." Tangie shrugged. "It's just. . .both of you are married now. And I'm. . ."

"You're the next big Broadway sensation," Taffie said with a smile.

"No, I'm not." Tangie sat, her sky blue dress billowing around her in a fluffy cloudlike circle. "I'm going to go on doing goofy shows in small theaters for the rest of my life. Who's going to want to marry sweet Nell?"

"I said the same thing two years ago," Taffie said. "I couldn't imagine who would want to marry me. Then God brought Ryan."

"And you know me," Candy added. "I was convinced I'd be single forever. And now Darren and I. . ." A lump formed in her throat. "Anyway, I was wrong, and I'm happy to admit it. And you're wrong, too."

Their mother drew near and wrapped Tangie in her arms. "Honey, don't you fret about who you'll marry. . .or when. I've been praying for all of you since you were children, that God would bring just the right mate. Now that my prayers have been answered for both of your sisters, I have more time to focus on you. And you know what a prayer warrior I am. Why, I'll pray in your real Dudley Do-Right in no time. Watch and see."

Tangie laughed. "Okay. Well, just make sure he likes girls who are. . .different."

"You're not different, honey. You're just you. And you're the very best you, you can possibly be. When the fellow I've been praying for lays eyes on my darling baby girl, he's going to see you for who you are. . .inside and out."

"Thanks, Mama." She sniffled. "I feel better."

Brooke reached for a tissue and dabbed at her eyes. "You

Carinis are so. . .emotional. You're not making this easy on me. I'm pregnant, you know."

"Yes, we know," they all echoed in chorus.

A knock on the door startled them back to attention. Candy looked up at the clock once more. Yikes. 1:58.

"Candy?" her father called out.

"Come in, Pop. We're ready for you."

He entered the room, a smile lighting his face the moment he laid eyes on her. She glanced at him and smiled. "Yes?"

"Cotton Candy." He gave her a wink.

"You're not going to say I have my head in the clouds are you, Pop? 'Cause if you are—"

"No." His eyes misted over. "You've definitely got your feet on the ground. Well, at least in matters of the heart. I was going to say. . ." His eyes misted over. "I was going to say you're the prettiest bride I've ever seen."

"Dad, I distinctly remember hearing you say that to me on my wedding day," Taffie said.

"Well, yes." He shrugged.

"And you're going to say it to me on my wedding day, too, right?" Tangie added.

He shrugged. "Of course." He turned his attention back to Candy. "But honey. . .today, standing here, you're the prettiest bride that ever walked the aisle. And I mean that from the bottom of my heart." He leaned over and whispered, "Just don't tell your mama I said that. She looked mighty good on our big day, too."

"I heard that, Carl." Their mother leaned over and gave him a peck on the cheek. "But I forgive you. And besides, I think you're right. We've got the prettiest—and the sweetest—girls who ever walked an aisle. Er, *runway*."

Candy chuckled, then gasped as she looked at the clock. Two o'clock? Better get this show on the road!

❧

Darren paced the lobby of the small airport, staring at the

clock on the wall. Two o'clock. Yikes. Better get going. Guests were waiting. Over one hundred and fifty of them, from what he'd been told.

As Darren, Jimmy, Jason, and Ryan made their way toward the runway, he stared at the setup, amazed. "I still can't believe this. It's. . .perfect."

"Yeah, I wasn't sure what to expect when the event planners showed up with the chairs and decorations," Jimmy said. "Never threw a wedding on a runway before. But I think the gazebo area looks great up at the front. And that runner gives the impression of an aisle. You've got to admit. . .it's different."

"It's different all right. But so are we." Darren smiled, then turned to Jimmy. "I can't thank you enough for shutting things down long enough for the wedding. You, um, *did* shut things down, right? No traffic on our runway during the ceremony?"

"No traffic on *any* runway during the wedding," Jimmy assured him.

"Thank you. I owe you big time." Darren took his place at the front next to Pastor Richardson, from their church. The other guys headed to the area in the back to meet up with their bridesmaids.

As he settled into place at the front of the crowd, Darren looked to the front row where his parents sat together holding hands. Wow. Talk about progress. His mother flashed a smile, and he responded by mouthing, "I love you." He then watched as she reached for a tissue. My, how things had changed. He could hardly wait to see what God had planned for the next phase of their journey.

As the piped-in music began to play, Darren thought about all of the changes the past few months had brought. He'd officially proposed to Candy onboard a flight to Chicago in front of ninety-seven passengers. Thankfully, she had agreed. Again. He'd also purchased the Cessna 208 from a friend of Jimmy's and routinely flew back and forth between D.C. and New York, carrying some pretty well-known political types. . .thanks to

Andrea Jackson and her new fiancé, a great guy named Marcus who worked for FOX News. And she promised him even more business in the future, particularly if Paul Cromwell made his run for the presidency. Maybe, before long, Darren would own a whole fleet of planes, hire pilots to fly for him. Perhaps the best news of all. . .a subdued, repentant Gary had recently approached him, asking for a job. Darren had promised to pray about it.

But right now he had other things to pray about.

He watched as the bridesmaids made their way up the makeshift aisle in their blue dresses with groomsmen at their side.

Brooke came first on her husband's arm. Darren had to laugh every time he remembered their announcement about the baby. Jason was about to become a father, whether he'd planned for it or not. And he'd be a great one.

Next came Taffie on Ryan's arm. They had a lot to celebrate these days, now that little Maddy was in the picture. And they beamed with joy on this special day.

Tangie entered last on Jimmy's arm. He could hardly believe the transformation. She looked. . .normal. No piercings. No orange hair. No tattoos. At least not any visible ones. And Jimmy grinned like a Cheshire cat.

Finally the long-awaited moment came. As Candy, on her father's arm, stepped out from behind the makeshift wall at the rear of the aisle, Darren gasped. Her white dress was perfect. She looked like something out of a magazine.

*Oh, Candy, just wait. I'm going to fly you to places you've never seen before. Like Italy, for instance. Tomorrow.*

Another glance her way and his hands started trembling. She took steps in his direction, a confident smile on her face. As she drew near, he was better able to see the details of her dress. With the brilliant blue sky in the background, her billowing white gown looked as pretty as a cloud. . .a cotton candy cloud.

# twenty-three

Candy watched as her sisters walked out onto the runway ahead of her. Off in the distance, she saw the Cessna 208, Darren's new charter plane. Once the ceremony ended, the two of them would climb aboard and fly off into the sunset. Just like a scene from a movie, only with a real, God-created backdrop. No more flight of fancy. No more pretending. This was the real deal.

She glanced up at the sky. It was a brilliant blue with white cumulus clouds hanging like fluffs of cotton candy. "Just for me, Lord. Thanks for the reminder."

The sound of the bridal march brought her attention back to the wedding.

"You ready, Cotton Candy?" Her pop gazed down at her with tenderness in his eyes.

"Yep. Let's get this plane off the ground."

The next twenty minutes passed like a whirlwind. She vaguely remembered Pastor Richardson's introduction. Heard the beautiful song that her sisters sang. Saw the tears in Darren's eyes as they took their vows. Felt the presence of the Lord as they shared their first kiss as a married couple. Heard the cheers from the crowd as the pastor introduced them as man and wife.

What stood out the most, however, was the feeling of pure joy that wrapped her like a blanket throughout the ceremony...a God-breathed joy. And by the time the pictures were taken and the guests convened in the hangar for the reception, she truly felt as if she were walking on a cloud. The whole thing had been simply breathtaking. Fast, but breathtaking.

As things began to slow down, she finally managed to get a good look at the hangar, completely overwhelmed at the transformation. She wouldn't have believed it if she hadn't seen it with her own eyes, but the wedding coordinator was right. . .the tent they'd erected inside the large space did the trick. It gave the room a cozy, elegant feel. Ribbons of blue satin hung in strips above the room, giving a sky-like effect. And the decorations! How fun to see Darren's model planes in use once again.

*It's perfect! I couldn't have dreamed up anything better.*

While she and Darren shared their first dance, she finally had a few minutes to whisper words of love into his ear. He responded with misty eyes and a promise to love her, whatever circumstance life brought their way. With God at the helm, they certainly had the promise of wonderful, adventurous days ahead.

After a great meal, the time came to cut the cake. Ice cream cake, of course. Candy had her mother to thank for that. And the wedding taffy! The guests ate it up and asked for more. Looked like the Carinis had outdone themselves this time around. Nothing new there.

When the reception ended, the moment arrived. The one she'd been longing for and dreading all at the same time. Instead of driving off in a car, she and Darren had—naturally—opted to fly off in his new 208. It wasn't the fear of flying that made her breath catch in her throat. No, it was something else entirely.

Candy and Darren changed into their going-away clothes, said their good-byes, then headed hand in hand to the plane.

He looked up at the plane, a look of pure contentment on his face. "I can't believe she's ours."

"The first in our brood." Candy gave him a wink.

They climbed aboard the plane, and Darren turned to her, a look of surprise on his face when he noticed Jimmy in the pilot's seat.

"Wait." Darren turned to Candy, confused. "I definitely don't think we need three pilots here. What's going on?"

Her hands shook with excitement as she explained. "Well, um, there's something I need to tell you. Sort of a wedding surprise." *Help me, Lord!*

"O–okay." He looked at her, clearly confused.

She tried to keep her voice steady as she spoke. "I think it's time I made the jump."

"We just did." The confusion on his face remained for a moment, then morphed into understanding. "Oh, do you mean. . .are you saying what I think you're saying?"

She nodded, though she could feel the color draining from her face as Jimmy handed them their chutes. Her knees started knocking and her hands shaking. "But we'd better do this now, or I'm going to change my mind."

"Oh no you're not!" He helped her into her chute, then prepared his own, offering up a celebratory prayer all the while.

With Jimmy at the helm, the small plane made its ascent into the beautiful blue skies. Cotton candy clouds beckoned, and at just the right moment, with friends and family looking on, Candy and Darren made their first leap together. . .into the vast unknown.

# A Letter To Our Readers

Dear Reader:
In order that we might better contribute to your reading enjoyment, we would appreciate your taking a few minutes to respond to the following questions. We welcome your comments and read each form and letter we receive. When completed, please return to the following:

Fiction Editor
Heartsong Presents
PO Box 719
Uhrichsville, Ohio 44683

1. Did you enjoy reading *Cotton Candy Clouds* by Janice Hanna?
   ❑ Very much! I would like to see more books by this author!
   ❑ Moderately. I would have enjoyed it more if

   _____
   _____
   _____

2. Are you a member of **Heartsong Presents**? ❑ Yes ❑ No
   If no, where did you purchase this book? _____

   _____

3. How would you rate, on a scale from 1 (poor) to 5 (superior), the cover design? _____

4. On a scale from 1 (poor) to 10 (superior), please rate the following elements.

   ____ Heroine          ____ Plot
   ____ Hero             ____ Inspirational theme
   ____ Setting          ____ Secondary characters

5. These characters were special because? _____
   _____
   _____

6. How has this book inspired your life? _____
   _____
   _____

7. What settings would you like to see covered in future
   **Heartsong Presents** books? _____
   _____
   _____

8. What are some inspirational themes you would like to see
   treated in future books? _____
   _____
   _____

9. Would you be interested in reading other **Heartsong
   Presents** titles? ❏ Yes  ❏ No

10. Please check your age range:
    ❏ Under 18          ❏ 18-24
    ❏ 25-34             ❏ 35-45
    ❏ 46-55             ❏ Over 55

Name_____
Occupation _____
Address _____
City, State, Zip_____

*Dear Reader,*

*I had always wanted to write a story about a female pilot flying for a small regional airline out of Newark, New Jersey.* Cotton Candy Clouds *gave me that opportunity. It was penned in 2008, several months before the night of February 12, 2009, when Continental Flight 3407 went down on her flight out of Newark. I was heartsick to receive the news. My thoughts and prayers are with the families and friends of those onboard.*

*Janice Hanna*

# Heartsong

**Any 12 Heartsong Presents titles for only $27.00***

## CONTEMPORARY ROMANCE IS CHEAPER BY THE DOZEN!

**Buy any assortment of twelve *Heartsong Presents* titles and save 25% off the already discounted price of $2.97 each!**

*plus $4.00 shipping and handling per order and sales tax where applicable.
If outside the U.S. please call
740-922-7280 for shipping charges.

## HEARTSONG PRESENTS TITLES AVAILABLE NOW:

___HP581  *Love Online*, K. Billerbeck
___HP582  *The Long Ride Home*, A. Boeshaar
___HP585  *Compassion's Charm*, D. Mills
___HP586  *A Single Rose*, P. Griffin
___HP589  *Changing Seasons*, C. Reece and J. Reece-Demarco
___HP590  *Secret Admirer*, G. Sattler
___HP593  *Angel Incognito*, J. Thompson
___HP594  *Out on a Limb*, G. Gaymer Martin
___HP597  *Let My Heart Go*, B. Huston
___HP598  *More Than Friends*, T. H. Murray
___HP601  *Timing is Everything*, T. V. Bateman
___HP602  *Dandelion Bride*, J. Livingston
___HP605  *Picture Imperfect*, N. J. Farrier
___HP606  *Mary's Choice*, Kay Cornelius
___HP609  *Through the Fire*, C. Lynxwiler
___HP613  *Chorus of One*, J. Thompson
___HP614  *Forever in My Heart*, L. Ford
___HP617  *Run Fast, My Love*, P. Griffin
___HP618  *One Last Christmas*, J. Livingston
___HP621  *Forever Friends*, T. H. Murray
___HP622  *Time Will Tell*, L. Bliss
___HP625  *Love's Image*, D. Mayne
___HP626  *Down From the Cross*, J. Livingston
___HP629  *Look to the Heart*, T. Fowler
___HP630  *The Flat Marriage Fix*, K. Hayse
___HP633  *Longing for Home*, C. Lynxwiler
___HP634  *The Child Is Mine*, M. Colvin
___HP637  *Mother's Day*, J. Livingston
___HP638  *Real Treasure*, T. Davis
___HP641  *The Pastor's Assignment*, K. O'Brien
___HP642  *What's Cooking*, G. Sattler
___HP645  *The Hunt for Home*, G. Aiken
___HP649  *4th of July*, J. Livingston
___HP650  *Romanian Rhapsody*, D. Franklin
___HP653  *Lakeside*, M. Davis
___HP654  *Alaska Summer*, M. H. Flinkman
___HP657  *Love Worth Finding*, C. M. Hake

___HP658  *Love Worth Keeping*, J. Livingston
___HP661  *Lambert's Code*, R. Hauck
___HP665  *Bah Humbug, Mrs. Scrooge*, J. Livingston
___HP666  *Sweet Charity*, J. Thompson
___HP669  *The Island*, M. Davis
___HP670  *Miss Menace*, N. Lavo
___HP673  *Flash Flood*, D. Mills
___HP677  *Banking on Love*, J. Thompson
___HP678  *Lambert's Peace*, R. Hauck
___HP681  *The Wish*, L. Bliss
___HP682  *The Grand Hotel*, M. Davis
___HP685  *Thunder Bay*, B. Loughner
___HP686  *Always a Bridesmaid*, A. Boeshaar
___HP689  *Unforgettable*, J. L. Barton
___HP690  *Heritage*, M. Davis
___HP693  *Dear John*, K. V. Sawyer
___HP694  *Riches of the Heart*, T. Davis
___HP697  *Dear Granny*, P. Griffin
___HP698  *With a Mother's Heart*, J. Livingston
___HP701  *Cry of My Heart*, L. Ford
___HP702  *Never Say Never*, L. N. Dooley
___HP705  *Listening to Her Heart*, J. Livingston
___HP706  *The Dwelling Place*, K. Miller
___HP709  *That Wilder Boy*, K. V. Sawyer
___HP710  *To Love Again*, J. L. Barton
___HP713  *Secondhand Heart*, J. Livingston
___HP714  *Anna's Journey*, N. Toback
___HP717  *Merely Players*, K. Kovach
___HP718  *In His Will*, C. Hake
___HP721  *Through His Grace*, K. Hake
___HP722  *Christmas Mommy*, T. Fowler
___HP725  *By His Hand*, J. Johnson
___HP726  *Promising Angela*, K. V. Sawyer
___HP729  *Bay Hideaway*, B. Loughner
___HP730  *With Open Arms*, J. L. Barton
___HP733  *Safe in His Arms*, T. Davis
___HP734  *Larkspur Dreams*, A. Higman and J. A. Thompson

(If ordering from this page, please remember to include it with the order form.)

# Presents

## Great Inspirational Romance at a Great Price!

**Heartsong Presents** books are inspirational romances in contemporary and historical settings, designed to give you an enjoyable, spirit-lifting reading experience. You can choose wonderfully written titles from some of today's best authors like Wanda E. Brunstetter, Mary Conneuly, Susan Page Davis, Cathy Marie Hake, Joyce Livingston, and many others.

*When ordering quantities less than twelve, above titles are $2.97 each.*
*Not all titles may be available at time of order.*